"I love you," he said. "I always have. I always will."

She stopped dead in her tracks. She wasn't sure she'd heard him correctly, and she didn't have the nerve to ask him to repeat himself.

Zach strode behind her and touched her hair. "But the facts don't change. If you stay you'll be used as a pawn or worse by the D.A. or by your family. You'll be in danger." He gripped her shoulders and turned her to face him. Intently he looked into her eyes. "And you have to leave, because if you stay...I can't stop myself from wanting you, from wanting you to be my wife. And if you are, think of the alliances that will be forged. How we'll be used, how our children could be used."

In a moment of blinding clarity, she understood.

"I wish I had a lifetime to give you," he said. "I wish I had at least one night to make love to you, but all I can give you now is a kiss."

ABOUT THE AUTHOR

Vivian Leiber was a Chicago trial attorney for many years before pursuing her first and truest love—writing. She lives in the North Shore of Chicago, among people very much like the ones she writes about. She has two adult children and two younger boys who are just wild enough to be a lot of fun.

Books by Vivian Leiber

HARLEQUIN INTRIGUE
416—HIS KIND OF TROUBLE

HARLEQUIN AMERICAN ROMANCE
576—BABY MAKES NINE
640—BLUE-JEANED PRINCE
655—MARRYING NICKY
672—A MILLION-DOLLAR MAN
686—ALWAYS A HERO
712—AN ORDINARY DAY

His Betrothed
Vivian Leiber

Harlequin Books

TORONTO • NEW YORK • LONDON
AMSTERDAM • PARIS • SYDNEY • HAMBURG
STOCKHOLM • ATHENS • TOKYO • MILAN
MADRID • WARSAW • BUDAPEST • AUCKLAND

This book is dedicated to Denise, who has to have a lot of faith and a lot of energy to work with me; to Officer Bob Kerner, who never hesitates to tell me the real story behind the story; and my two boys—Joseph and Eastman, thank you for taking Mommy's manuscript to the post office.

ISBN 0-373-22460-5

HIS BETROTHED

Copyright © 1998 by Arlynn Leiber Presser

Printed in U.S.A.

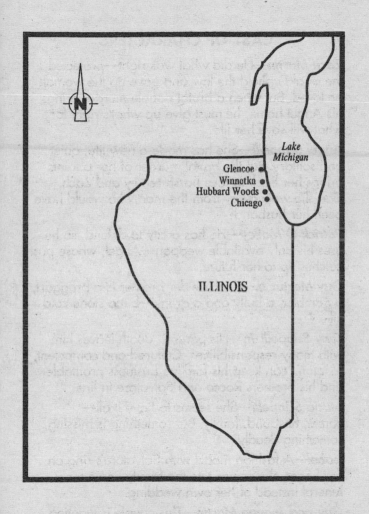

Lake
Michigan

Glencoe •
Winnotka •
Hubbard Woods •
Chicago •

ILLINOIS

CAST OF CHARACTERS

Zach Martin—He did what was right—protected the weak, upheld the law and gave up the woman he loved. But when a brutal double murder brings his Angel home, he must give up what's right for what will save her life.

Angel Sciopelli—She has made a new life, quiet and solitary. But the brutal murder of her parents brings her back to face harsh reality and Zach. Can she walk away from the man who would have been her husband?

Patrick O'Malley—He has a city to defend, so he uses his only available weapon—Angel, whose past catches up to her future.

Guy Martin Jr.—Zach's elder brother is a braggart, a gambler, a bully and a drunk—but a stone-cold killer?

Tony Sciopelli Jr.—His parents' death leaves him with many responsibilities. Cultured and competent, he alone can keep his family's business profitable and his brothers Rocco and Salvatore in line.

Maria Sciopelli—She seems to have it all—career, husband, family. But something is missing, something deadly.

Isabel—A fashion model with Salvatore's ring on her finger, she comes into the family home for a funeral instead of her own wedding.

Guy and Jeanne Martin—This couple is wanting for nothing. Except maybe revenge.

Prologue

"Angel, I don't think this is a good idea," Zach said, glancing back at the Sciopelli house. As her fingers tugged him, he felt her gold ring studded with peridot and citrine, their birthstones, against his palm. He had given her the ring this evening, after the prom, knowing that the more formal diamond should wait. But there was no question that she was his, had been promised to him on the day of her christening. But she was not his completely, he conceded, glancing back to the whitewashed Mediterranean stucco mansion again.

The light from her father's second-story window was bright and accusatory.

Zach was brought back to the pleasures of the night by the image of Angel in the moonlight. A sheath of white silk dipped scandalously over her high, swelling breasts and nipped in at her tiny waist before billowing to gossamer light clouds that ended at her beribboned silver slippers. She had begun the evening with her buttery blond hair pulled back into a severe and complicated style studded with pearls, but now, as he reached down to pick up a pearl pin that had come undone, waves of flaxen caressed his fingers.

As he rose, he came face-to-face with Angel, her hands on hips, pale blue eyes luminous and large.

"Are you saying you don't want to?"

"Of course I do. You know that."

"Well, I do, too. I'm a high school graduate now. You don't have to treat me like a child. And besides, Zach, we're nearly married." She jabbed her finger at him playfully.

"There's a difference between nearly and married," Zach said, feeling his reasoning tumbling down a slippery slope into raw animal action. "Your father trusts me. He always has. I can't break that trust."

Her eyes were smoky from tiredness and longing. Her mouth, full and pouting, shiny and ready for him. He was aware that he, at twenty-one and a man, had suffered his share of restless nights and cold showers. But Angel was just coming into her sexual moment—her feelings were new and as confusing and frightening as any frontier. He felt protective toward her.

But then again, he always had.

"Zach," she whispered, in just that way she had, the way that made his defenses crumble. "I'm not a child anymore. I want to be a woman. Your woman."

"You shouldn't push me like this," Zach warned.

But she pushed him, utterly and completely to his limit. And when her hand reached into the black-as-midnight dinner jacket with a boldness that neither would have ever expected her to possess, he was un-done. And she didn't back off.

"Angel," he moaned.

"Come with me," she whispered bewitchingly.

Through darkness punctuated by fireflies, Angel Sciopelli led Zach down the lily-scented garden path to the pool cabana. The pool was illuminated, water vapor rising like magician's smoke. She pulled him into the terra-cotta dressing area, its familiar smell of chlorine reminding him of all the stolen kisses of their childhood, all the times he would have, could have—but didn't because she was Angel, special, in-nocent and as precious as a bride should be.

Besides, their fathers had made a promise on her christening day when he was just four. And Zach knew that he'd be a fool to lose her.

"Tell me you're not like them," she said, giving just the barest nod in the direction of the house be-fore tugging at her dress.

He glanced at the house, its many levels lit by

dramatic garden lights. He wondered at her question, so peculiar. She adored her father and worshipped her three brothers—Angel would like nothing better than to believe that all of the men in her life were essentially of the same high character.

But all thought stopped as her dress fell to the ground. She stood before him in a pale bra and stockings, a garter belt that secured shimmering sheer stockings. She looked as knowing as a lingerie catalog model and, paradoxically, as unsure of herself as the virgin she was.

"Tell me," she repeated with unaccountable passion. "Tell me you're not like them."

He wondered briefly how much she knew and then shook his head. She couldn't have figured it out. It had taken him nearly a year to understand himself.

"I'm not," he said. And he knew much of what he said was true. Much of it. "I'm not like them."

"I knew it," she said, smiling happily. "I knew it."

She knelt on the chaise, looking up at him. He could talk, he could ask her what she meant or he could take her. And while another man might choose differently, Zach was young and he had waited so long, so long.

He tugged off his bow tie, undid the pearl buttons of his pleated shirt and then and only then allowed himself to touch her. He began with a kiss, listened to her soft sigh, and then trailed a rough but re-strained hand along the base of her neck, pausing at the jumping pulse before he continued. There was no turning back for either of them.

He felt his pleasure as much in guiding her to new peaks as he did in satisfying his own need to possess her.

Afterward, they lay spoonwise on the chaise.

"We have to leave," she said, her voice startling him from a moment of rare calm. "I heard them talking—your father and mine—earlier today. It was about the indictment."

The word sounded coarse and vulgar as she said it.

"What do you know about any indictment?"

"I read the papers," she said smartly. "I went to my father's study to ask him about it. At the door, just before I knocked, I heard the two of them. My father said it would end—" Her voice broke with emotion. "He said it would end with either him or O'Malley, the state's attorney, in the grave."

Zach stiffened. This was more than she should know. Much more.

"Then what happened?" he asked neutrally.

"I walked in and asked my father to explain," Angel replied. "He said that the building trades have always been the target of government interference. He said that years ago, the Mafia had its hand in so many different construction companies and unions that a regular businessman had suspicion cast upon him even when he didn't deserve it.''

"And was that enough?'' Zach questioned her with deceptive casualness.

"No,'' Angel said vehemently. "And I can't believe I was such a fool, never knowing where all this came from.''

"What do you mean...all this?''

"The house, the clothes, the private schooling, the red Corvette he got me as a graduation present. I've lived a very good life, Zach, but I've done so at the expense of what's right.''

Zach chose his next words with care.

"Your father owns a company that builds things.''

"But that's not where this money comes from. He uses the legitimate business to shield other, less legitimate enterprises. Like money laundering, gambling...I don't even want to think about the rest.''

"You don't think he's an honest contractor?''

"No,'' Angel said bluntly.

He couldn't see her face now, but he could feel her tension. It matched his own.

"Do you believe he's honest?''

"No,'' Zach confessed. As much as he knew it would be better to lie, he couldn't. His feelings were still too raw, too vivid, about her father.

"Then you'll leave with me, won't you?''

"Where are you going?" he asked with alarm.

"Anywhere. Someplace. I don't know where. But I can't stay here. You're going with me, aren't you? You must have been staying all this time because you thought I was too young to leave. But now I'm old enough. And I'm your wife."

"We're not—"

"We are married," she insisted. "You made me your wife just now. Here in your arms. It's even more precious than a church ceremony."

"I...I can't leave."

"Whose side are you on?"

"Yours. Ours. The right side."

"Then you'll go with me. Your father's involved, too. You must know that. Every time Martin trucks deliver a load from a materials contractor to a Sciopelli site, they are reloaded with drugs, weapons, other contraband. Our fathers couldn't do it without each other."

"Yes. I know."

"Then let's go. Start a new life. Now. Tonight. Every day we stay is wrong."

Zach eased his body upright, kissed her shoulder and came to a decision.

"All right, we'll go," he said steadily.

Her relief and trust were palpable.

"Oh, Zach, I knew loving you was always right. That you're good and kind and strong, and I promise you you'll never regret going with me. We'll make a new life. All our own. I'll be a good wife to you. And I'll give you beautiful children."

They each thought of the future. She smiled radiantly, her face turned up to see the moonlight filtering from behind the birch trees. Zach ran his fingers through his hair, trying to forestall a headache.

"I'm sure you will be a good wife," he said. "Now, here's what we'll do. I'll buy us some plane tickets. Does Las Vegas sound good? We can get married there. I'll have the tickets waiting at the United counter at O'Hare airport. I've got some business to tie up, so you pick up your ticket and meet me on the plane. Deal?"

"Deal," she said, and leaned in the darkness to kiss him. He felt her tears—or were they his?—against his cheeks. And then, in an instant, she was dressed and gone, taking the scent of vanilla and baby powder with her. "Till tomorrow," she said with a last bit of hope and love and a kiss as sweet as cotton candy.

"Goodbye, Angel," he said, picking up the corsage that he had attached to her dress earlier. His fingers caressed the white roses and baby's breath. And then, in a swift and brutal gesture, he crushed the flowers in his hand and cursed the fates that had made him who he was.

Chapter One

It was a terrible day for a funeral, Zach Martin thought as he pulled the charcoal-colored suit jacket over his broad, muscular shoulders.

The afternoon was too sunny, too tantalizingly warm, too lush with shocking pink tulips and duckbill yellow daffodils blooming in abundance on the borders of the well-manicured lawn surrounding Chicago's Sacred Heart Cathedral.

A day for the living, not for the dead.

Raking a hand through his hair, Zach scanned the parade of long, sleek, jet black limousines depositing mourners at Sacred Heart's Gothic arched doors.

He locked his sporty red Camaro, wondering if Angel would...no, she wouldn't come, he told himself. He only allowed himself the briefest memory of Angel, the most beautiful woman he had ever known, the woman who had been promised to him in marriage and the only woman he had ever betrayed.

He tormented himself with the image of crystal-like aquamarine eyes. The clean scent of talc and vanilla. The sound of her voice as she said his name. The slender curve of her legs and the way her lips broke into a heart-stopping smile when she was truly happy. Her hair, long tender curls, warm blond in winter and sun-kissed white by the end of July.

His recollection was as vivid as the last moment he saw her, a flash of white cloudlike fabric skittering across the moonlit courtyard, running toward a future that she thought would include him.

She wouldn't come back today, he thought as he walked toward the church. Angel had never once come home for holidays, birthdays, weddings or christenings. Zach had graduated from college and then law school, been sworn to practice in the state and federal courts, had won his first major trial—all without his betrothed at his side. He never even knew where she was, although he knew that he had ways to find out.

But he had, with the discipline of a recovering alcoholic, never satisfied himself.

No, she wouldn't come to bury her parents.

She might not even know of her father's and mother's deaths, although the ambush at the posh restaurant after a meal meant to celebrate the ground-breaking for the new Winnetka Shopping Mall had been the lead story on several national news wire services. Zach had come to the dinner only out of obligation to his family and, by arriving late, he had been just in time to see the carnage.

Just in time to cradle Mrs. Sciopelli in his arms as her life ebbed. On the parkway around them, the Sciopelli brothers shouted contradictory orders and futilely called for help.

Luckily Maria and Isabel hadn't even arrived for the dinner yet and were to be spared the sight of Papa and Mama Sciopelli dying scant yards from each other.

"Oh, Zach," Mrs. Sciopelli had moaned in Zach's arms. "Protect my little Angel."

She had never said a word to him in all the years since Angel left. But he suspected, in those final moments, that she knew the truth of why he had stayed.

"I will," he promised her. "I always have and I always will."

She was satisfied, as satisfied as she had been when he had stood, four years old and wearing a tie for the first time, at the wicker bassinet, staring at the most beautiful baby in the world. His Angel. She had fretted in her long christening gown, had grasped his finger and cooed. And he had fallen in love.

"You protect my little Angel," Mrs. Sciopelli had said, picking up her daughter and taking Zach's hand to walk to the garden where the party was gathering for the blessing.

"I will," he had promised solemnly, proudly holding the trail of lace on the christening gown's hem, convinced that when the Sciopelli guests looked in his direction, they did so because they recognized a formidable guardian and protector for the young baby.

On the steps of a swank Glencoe restaurant, satisfied with his final and enduring promise, Mrs. Sciopelli had died. She never asked about her husband.

Zach walked up the block, past a sprawling English Tudor mansion that served as Sacred Heart's rectory, through the subdued mourners gathering at the steps of the cathedral. He scanned the rooftops and doorways of the shops along busy Tower Road.

Aside from the television cameras covering the event for the evening news, the feds manned a video camera on the roof of the dry cleaner. Zach recognized a pair of FBI plainclothes scribbling notes from behind the shutters of the bakery window. Lurking near the uniformed officer directing traffic at the cathedral's entrance were three others taking down license plate numbers. By day's end, a photo album of mourners would be available for any law enforcement official who needed it.

Even the flowers that graced the inside of the church would be photographed by the feds as soon as the mourners left for the grave-side service. Those photos would be studied and puzzled over—who sent the largest arrangement, where the arrangements were placed and, God forbid, if any yellow flowers were sent.

Yellow flowers were a mark of betrayal and enmity.

Zach paused at the steps of the cathedral, letting the sun fall flush upon his face. Waiting until he was sure that the cameraman hidden behind the curtains of the deli across the street could snap a few shots. Giving in to a mischievous impulse, Zach waved. He didn't want any misunderstandings later.

He was here at the funeral—he made no excuses for himself. He stepped into the dark, cool, marble-floored cathedral. A choir of young boys, perfectly pitched, sang "Regina, Queen of Heaven" from behind a tapestry screen placed on the right side of the sacristy.

Two glistening polished mahogany caskets were placed in front of the richly appointed altar. The steps surrounding the altar were crowded by a cascade of brilliant colored flowers.

Not a yellow flower in sight.

The Martin family was seated in the pew directly behind Tony Sciopelli, Jr., his wife, Maria, and his two younger brothers, Rocco and Salvatore. He nodded to each of them in turn. He kissed Maria's cool cheek and awkwardly repeated the ritual with Isabel, Salvatore's fiancée. She had been a guest of the Sciopellis for just the past month and the double murder would no doubt put off their wedding date.

As he surveyed the Sciopellis, Zach realized with a start that he had unconsciously thought he would find Angel in the pew where her family was seated.

If they had married, she would have been there. If they had married, the Martin and Sciopelli families would have been forever joined through their children. That was what her father had wanted, what his father had promised for him. And denying them their wish was the first of many betrayals Zach had made.

Because he knew that to marry Angel would have been wrong, a betrayal to what was right.

"Darling, we were worried you wouldn't make it," Jeanne Martin whispered, making room for him in the pew. He sat beside his mother and she leaned over to kiss his cheek. Her perfume was an expensive oriental, her black silk shantung suit Dior, but her eyes were worn and tired.

Still, she was the most beautiful woman in the cathedral, even if Salvatore's fiancée was supposed to be a famous runway model in Italy.

His mother touched the scar on his cheek. Funny, as if she were surprised by it every time she saw him. A scrape with a bunch of neighborhood toughs who had been relentlessly bullying his brother, Guy, Jr. Though Zach was younger by two years than Guy and his tormenters, he had charged. His ferocious defense of Guy had brought peace for his brother and a razor-thin white line on Zach's cheek.

"Ma, it's not going away," he said.

She smiled. It was their private joke.

"It saves you from being too handsome," she said, gently rubbing it.

Zach nodded hello to his father, Guy Martin, Sr., who coughed a reply. He looked worse than he had a week ago, when Zach had seen him last. The death of his colleague and friend had taken its toll.

Guy, Jr., held out his hand. His puffy fingers trembled—Zach guessed his brother's distress was due to the fact that it was already twelve-thirty in the afternoon and drinks hadn't been served.

"Hey, Zach," Guy whispered. "Good to see you. Sorry about you bein' there and all."

"You weren't at the dinner?"

"I was. But I was inside. I didn't get out there until it was damn near over. But I heard you helped her...at the end. I saw you going in the ambulance with her, though I guess she was already gone."

Zach nodded.

"How's Anna?" he asked, quietly so that no one would hear.

Of course, Anna would be at home, at the imposing Georgian mansion on the estate overlooking Lake Michigan. Anna never appeared in public, except for the increasingly rare afternoons that Zach was able to take off work to treat her to a movie, the zoo, the circus.

Some people had even forgotten that Zach had a younger sister, which was how his father would prefer it.

"Maria lent me her housekeeper to baby-sit her."

"That was very nice."

"But you haven't been so nice. Why did you have to buy her the Barbie Malibu Beach House?" his mother whispered with mock severity. "She's put real sand all over her bedroom floor to make it more realistic."

Zach shrugged. "At least she likes it."

The last soaring notes of the hymn echoed through the palatial church. Bishop John Ferrigan, dressed in the sumptuous robes of his office, called for a moment of silent reflection.

Zach crossed himself, but before he could close his eyes in prayer a flicker of movement behind the side altar to Saint Joseph caught his attention. He stared, puzzled, and then the figure, dressed barely suitable in rumpled mourning, peered at him from behind the shadows.

O'Malley.

Wanting to believe the best of him, Zach assumed the hunter had feelings of respect for the prey that had been taken down so brutally by another. But it could just as well be that O'Malley was working, storing up even more information about the two families he had worked so hard to bring down.

Still, being here was a risk. The D.A. wasn't welcome.

Before Zach could make any acknowledgment, the shadow was swallowed by the darkness of the Saint Joseph sanctuary and Zach wondered if he had only imagined O'Malley's presence.

He'd have to ask him about it later.

Zach closed his eyes and his thoughts fell into the cadence set by the bishop. He whispered the familiar words of comfort and hope for the dead. Then he heard an audible murmur at the back of the cathedral.

His mother turned around, the brim of her straw hat brushing against his ear.

"Oh, heavens!" she cried.

In the row ahead of them, Rocco muttered an oath and was quickly shushed by Tony, Jr.

"Our prayers have been answered at last," Salvatore exclaimed.

"What is *she* doing here?" Zach's brother, Guy, demanded.

"She came," his father wheezed triumphantly. "I knew she would come. She was always a good daughter. And I, for one, have missed her."

Zach didn't need to turn around. His heart soared even as he shook his head.

Trouble.

ANGEL SCIOPELLI LET the heavy oak door swing shut behind her, suppressing a shiver as the cool, damp air of the cathedral enveloped her. She blinked twice and reached to take off her oversize dark tortoiseshell glasses. Then she noticed the people.

A few hundred, maybe more, attended the double funeral for the Sciopellis and, although Sacred Heart Cathedral was the largest in the northern suburbs of Chicago, the pews were filled.

Everyone had swiveled around, necks craning, to look at her. The expressions on their faces ran the gamut from disdain to disgust.

Angel did a quick inventory of herself. In the taxi from Chicago's Palmer House Hotel, she had brushed her waist-length blond hair to a glistening sheen. Her black heels were higher than the sneakers she ordinarily wore to her job as a preschool teacher, but not so spiky that anyone could disapprove. Her stockings were dark and sheer—but she wouldn't give anyone the satisfaction of checking for runs now. Her black linen shift cut just at her knees didn't have too many wrinkles considering its long wear, and the matching straw envelope purse was classic and conservative.

The looks she garnered had nothing to do with some flaw in her appearance and everything to do with her merely showing up.

She shoved her sunglasses firmly on the bridge of

her nose, wishing she could take them off because her eyes were having trouble adjusting to the gray, murky lighting of the sanctuary.

But she needed the protection that the huge frames gave her—no one must see her fear.

As she stood uncertainly, something across her right shoulder caught her eye. She looked down the row of richly carved marble columns.

An old man, his dark suit swallowed by shadow, his face burnished by the light cast through red stained glass. He stepped backward, pressing himself against the wall of a confessional.

Still, she recognized him from the picture on the front page of her morning paper.

District Attorney Patrick O'Malley.

"It will end with him or me in the grave," her father had said.

And so it had, Angel thought grimly. She wondered if O'Malley were here as a measure of his respect or of his triumph.

Stepping out into the light, O'Malley stared at her with frank curiosity. She stared back. Then he smiled, an odd thing to do at a funeral and a gesture she did not return.

Then he walked away, his heels tap-tap-tapping on the marble floor.

She forced herself to look down the aisle where once she had thought she would walk as a bride. She looked to the two caskets side by side in front of the sacristy and, swaying, she came face-to-face with the finality of her parents' deaths. What had only been a news story on page one of her morning paper now became a real and visceral truth.

She scooted into the back most pew, which had a single open spot. Then Angel crossed herself, said a quick prayer and sat down, opening her funeral program. She looked up once to see her brother Tony standing in his place at the front pew.

He beckoned with the barest motion of his wrist.

But she shook her head. She wanted to keep her distance, pay her respects and get on the next plane out of Chicago.

He nodded, as if to say that he respected her choice, and sat down.

She didn't want to look, didn't want to be curious, didn't want to be interested, but she scanned the row behind Tony to find Zach. And she did. From behind, he looked taller, broader, more sure of himself, than she remembered, his hair darker than the blue-black crows that punctuated the farmland she now called home.

Seeing him—well, actually, seeing his back—for the first time in ten years, she experienced a long-dormant range of emotions. The disbelief. The grief. The endless questioning of herself, of him, of their love. Even, yes, the anger. And then the numbness.

And the determination that she would never, ever go through what she had endured when she had followed her conscience out of Chicago and assumed the man she thought of as her husband was going with her.

She put thoughts of him out of her head as Bishop Ferrigan began the service. Instead, she reflected upon her parents. Especially her innocent and beloved mother. If it weren't for her mother, she wouldn't have come.

Only when the service was over and the coffins had made their slow parade down the aisle did she look up, to see Zach Martin get up from the pew behind the last clump of mourners.

As he approached, she realized that he had grown in the past ten years. Grown not just in height and in musculature, but in the subtle confidence of manhood. Maybe it was better that he hadn't come with her because, frankly, he intimidated her.

And she didn't like to be intimidated.

"Hello, Zach," she said, playing it cool.

"Welcome home," Zach said with a courtly bow of his head. His scent was sure and masculine. "It's good to see you."

She willed herself not to look at him, fearing that the slightest weakening on her part would open the floodgates of desire and betrayal and questions that she had kept in check for ten long, excruciatingly lonely years.

"I'm not staying," she said firmly, putting her funeral program into her purse and snapping it shut.

"I'm sure you're a busy woman," he replied, and she noticed that he asked nothing about the intervening years.

"Yes, I am," she said, although the headmistress at the nursery school where she taught had said to take as long as she needed.

"Did you take a cab here? Would you like a ride to the cemetery?" he asked. "There will be a short service at the tomb."

"I don't think I'd be welcome."

"You will be if you're with me," he said confidently, and took her arm in his.

As he led her to the shiny red sports car parked up the block, Angel wondered what crimes he had committed, or had ordered committed, what bargains with the devil he had made. She reflected that there was an injustice that he could be so immoral and yet have the relaxed countenance of a man with a clear conscience.

His hair was sleek and shiny, maybe two weeks overdue on a cut. His eyes were clear, wreathed only by the lightest feather strokes of lines. His smile was broad, his teeth white and gleaming.

She decided it was terrible, truly terrible, to accept

favors from a man who had betrayed not just her but also the principles of what was right.

And yet she knew his strength, and she rued the fact that there was no one—no one she could name—upon whose arm she would be able to survive the gauntlet of relatives and family friends who had been ordered to consider her dead ten years before.

"Thank you," she said as he slid into the driver's seat beside her.

She knew her voice betrayed an impolite chill.

"My pleasure," he murmured as if he had not noticed her rebuff, and then he pulled the Camaro behind the slow-moving cortege.

Chapter Two

"Ashes to ashes, dust to dust."

Bishop Ferrigan shook the final droplets of holy water onto the two newest coffins to be placed in the Sciopelli burial chambers.

The tomb was an eight-foot-tall granite replica of the entrance to the Gangivecchio Abbey just outside Palermo. The stern marble cherub stooped on its roof bore both sword and shield, eternally guarding the remains of generations of Sciopellis.

Just inside the wrought-iron doorway, the pall-bearers—foremen of the Sciopelli Construction Company—awkwardly struggled to slide the two heavy caskets onto adjoining shelves.

That last piece of work for their boss accomplished, the men wiped the moss and spiderwebs from their hands and slipped back to their wives and families scattered throughout the crowd at the grave-side service.

The red-and-white robed altar boy closed and locked the door of the tomb. Bishop Ferrigan murmured the final prayers of the dead and, blessing the crowd, made a sign of the cross.

He then stepped aside for Tony, Jr., who placed two blood-red long-stemmed roses on the steps of his parents' final resting place. He crossed himself and, with the barest nod, silently granted his two younger brothers, Rocco and Salvatore, permission to approach the family tomb. Salvatore, thin and ethereally pale in sharp contrast to his robust brothers, pulled out a handkerchief and wiped away tears. Rocco yanked the two roses from his younger brother's hand and put them down on the moss-covered steps.

The three brothers stood together.

"Angel, come here," Tony called out, squinting against the sunlight. The clump of mourners turned to follow his gaze to Zach and Angel. Angel had chosen to stand in back so as not to draw attention to herself, but her strategy had backfired badly. "Come on, Angel, please. Make some room for our sister."

She stepped forward uncertainly and was borne along the wave of hesitant greetings and solemn handshakes from strangers and long-forgotten acquaintances.

Her hand was clasped by Tony's and he hoisted

her up the tomb's steps. Salvatore, who had played monopoly with her for two weeks straight when she got chicken pox, sobbed.

"It's all right, Salvatore," she said, as she had done so often when he was a child and suffered nightmares.

As he calmed in her embrace, she felt a familiar and long-denied love for him. Rocco stepped forward to awkwardly pat her back. He had always been the one to entertain her, putting on little puppet shows for her and slipping her out of the house to go to movies.

How could she believe these men, who were her own flesh and blood, were bad? How could she love men who did terrible things? Why didn't she judge them now as harshly as she had when she was seventeen and full of ideals?

It would be as if to believe that she herself was tainted in some way.

"It's all right, little sister," Rocco said. "We feel the same way, too."

But Angel knew Rocco misunderstood. Her tears were not for her parents—she had shed many tears for them, both before and after hearing of their deaths—but for the love she felt for her brothers. It was as strong as the day she alone got on the plane to Las Vegas—and as confused as ever.

"Welcome, Angel," Tony murmured. He pulled

her into a big bear hug. "We have missed you every single day for ten years. We're surprised to see you here."

She looked up at him, expecting to meet his eyes. But he looked beyond her, his baby blue eyes gone unexpectedly icy cold and calculating. She followed his gaze out beyond the crowd, as far as the clump of trees where Zach stood.

Zach's jaw tilted upward, a challenge.

"Come on back to the house with us," Tony purred, abruptly shifting gears. "I won't take no for an answer. We are family, Angel, and we have ten long years to catch up on."

"But I left because—"

"I know why you left," he whispered. "I know. But it was a long time ago, and our father was found innocent by a jury. Three times."

"Not guilty," Angel corrected. The verdicts for each of the three trials had been controversial.

"Same thing," he said, touching her lips to override her response. "We're not monsters, Angel, we're your brothers. And we're just businessmen trying to turn a profit in a tough market. Say you'll at least stop by the house. We can talk, can't we? We can show you the plans for the new Winnetka Shopping Mall—we have a scale model in the study. You'll see that we're so busy with this new project we couldn't do half the things Patrick O'Malley gives us credit for.''

Angel shook her head.

"I can't, Tony. I can't.''

He stiffened but said no more.

After a few moments of silence Bishop Ferrigan withdrew to his limousine. Tony led Rocco and Salvatore through the crowd, stopping occasionally for a handshake and a hug.

Tony's wife, Maria, who had been in Rocco's class in school, stepped forward to give her a kiss, leaving a waxy, ruby imprint that Angel wiped off her cheek with the back of her hand. Tall, lanky Isabel, who was introduced without explanation, gave her a puzzled look but dutifully kissed her cheek.

Angel swallowed hard, took in the blank stares of the mourners and stepped out of the way as discreetly as she knew how.

Guy Martin, Sr., the elder Sciopelli's closest friend, walked to the vault, with his wife and firstborn son holding tight to each of his arms.

"Angel, you have become such a beautiful woman," he said, withdrawing his arm from Guy, Jr., to place it squarely into Angel's care. "You have married, no?"

"No, I haven't, Mr. Martin.''

"Oh, so formal," he teased. "So no husband and no bambinos, huh?''

"No, none of that," Angel answered, helping him to place two red roses on the steps of the tomb. He stood apart from her for a moment, his grief making him look even older than his sixty years.

Then he motioned for Guy, Jr., to help him to his wheelchair and take him to the limousine.

"It's not too late for you and Zach," he croaked, squandering his last energy on his words.

She would have answered him, might have even told him that now wasn't a time to be thinking of marriage, but the conversation had cost him plenty. He slumped into his wheelchair and Guy wheeled him away.

As other mourners stepped up to offer their flowers, Angel walked in the direction of the cemetery gates.

"Can I take you anywhere?" Zach asked, slipping his hand into hers.

She pulled away.

They had not spoken a word during the short drive from the cathedral to the cemetery, but Angel wasn't sure that she could keep up the silent treatment all the way down to the city, to her hotel. She could say no, but there was the practical problem of being a mile and a half from the nearest train station.

She also had the sense that to say no would only provoke him, make him more insistent and stubborn.

And if she remembered one thing about Zach, it was that he got his way...or else.

"You can drop me off at the station," she suggested. "I've got to get back into the city."

"Good idea," he said.

He drove her directly to the train station, keeping up a spirited monologue about the prospects of the Chicago Cubs winning the pennant. She didn't make any comments and, thankfully, he didn't ask for any. He parked at the Hubbard Woods park across from the tracks. Angel got out and read the schedule taped to the station house window.

"Train's coming in ten minutes," she called out.

"I'll wait," Zach said, slamming shut the driver's side door.

"No, that's all right," Angel said. She sat down on the curbside bench and pulled a paperback out of her purse. "I'll be fine. I wanted to catch up on some reading. Thank you for the ride."

"But I could stay."

"I'm sure my brothers could use some company."

"The house will be filled with mourners."

"You can talk to the company so that my brothers can be alone."

"It's just another ten minutes."

"You've exhausted the topic of the Cubs," she informed him. "They don't win pennants, they win the hearts of their fans."

"We could talk about the weather, politics, religion, physics."

"You don't have ten minutes worth of physics in you. And I don't recall you having an interest in politics. And you always believed whatever the sisters taught you, so religion's out."

"That leaves weather. It's early June. Tornado weather. That's exciting."

This was the limit of her patience!

"No. Please, Zach, I want to be alone. Really alone."

She could have been no more effective at harming him than if she reached out and slapped him in the face. But he was at heart a stoic. His red flush diminished to the bronze of early-summer tan.

His startled eyes blinked twice and then became a placid and charming gray.

"I understand," he said with a courtly bow. "It's been a very rough time for you. So I guess it's time for goodbye."

He reached to kiss her cheek, but she turned her face away. He took the rebuff without comment and walked back to his car.

"Zach?"

"What?"

"Why?"

"Why what?"

She didn't want to ask, but she couldn't help herself. She had lived with the question unanswered for ten years. And she didn't have the self-control necessary to squelch the curiosity—and the need for closure.

"Why didn't you come? To the airport?"

"I don't think you really want to know the answer to that question."

"I can't help myself. I think about it way too much. Consider it a favor to me to just tell me flat-out why. You don't need to sugarcoat it."

The pain on his face was quick and sure. And so vital that Angel thought for a moment, a bare moment, that he felt the same way as she did. But then he shrugged, the instant of torment replaced with a rakish smile.

"It was a long time ago, Angel. We were kids, a couple a silly kids in the throes of puppy love. I hardly remember it clearly myself," he said with apparent ease. "I'm sorry if your feelings got hurt, but you look like you've done all right for yourself. And life goes on, right?"

Sucker punched by a stone-cold lover.

As he drove away in the Camaro, Angel stood at the curb, shocked into silence. Of all the stories she had told herself in the past ten years, this was not one of them. He was confused, she had said to herself. He feels loyalty to his father, she had told herself. He was simply not as in love with her as she was with him.

But never that he was this offhanded.

Puppy love? She might have been young, but her love for him was everything.

Well, he hadn't put any sugar on it!

Shaking her head, she watched the red Camaro until it was swallowed up in traffic on Green Bay Road.

She didn't see the black Pontiac sedan pull up to the curb until she felt the heat of the exhaust brush against her leg. The back smoked window eased down and a grizzled, gray face peered out.

"Ms. Sciopelli, I'm Patrick O'Malley," he said, his voice as choppy as if he were gargling rocks. "We need to talk."

"I know who you are from your picture in the paper," Angel said. "What were you doing at my parents' funeral?"

"I wanted to pay my respects."

"Sure."

"I have a certain respect, a certain bond, with your father, even if I don't like the things he did. Anyway, like I said, we need to talk."

"About what?"

"About the fact I need your help."

"No. I'm going home."

She stood and headed for the platform.

"Ms. Sciopelli," he called after her. "You're a teacher. You understand how important it is to think of the future of your children. To think about how to make a better world, one in which businessmen don't use their legitimate interests to hide the profits they make from kickbacks and extortion schemes."

She stopped in her tracks.

"How do you know I'm a teacher?" she asked.

He leaned out over the open window of the car.

"A district attorney has many sources of information," O'Malley replied easily. "Even in Davenport, Iowa. We know everything, Angel. Or should I call you Jennifer? Jennifer Smith is the name you've used for the past ten years, isn't it?"

A sudden rush of revulsion and dread swept through her.

"Why don't you get in the car?" he asked, and the driver got out and opened the passenger door on the other side of the car.

"Damn you, O'Malley" she said, surprising herself.

Her preschoolers had never heard her say anything more inflammatory than "fiddlesticks."

He shrugged. Obviously he had been called worse.

She sat as far away from him as she could, in the groove of black leather interior. A dark-suited man who offered no introduction sat on the jump seat across from them with an open notebook and a pencil. With no directions given, the driver pulled north on Green Bay Road. O'Malley placed a folder on the seat between himself and Angel.

"Here's your life, Angel," he said. She opened the first page to a birth certificate, a copy of the one she had purchased for herself ten years ago. "It's a nice life, Jennifer Smith. Preschool teacher. Playing piano for the church choir. Nice two bedroom apartment next to the bike path. A quiet life, keeping to yourself, not much in the way of dating. Some would say it's a little boring."

"I wouldn't."

"In any event, kiss it goodbye if you don't intend on cooperating."

She leafed through the file. It was all there. Photographs, canceled checks, bank statements— O'Malley knew more about her than anyone else on earth.

She closed the folder.

"So I left home and changed my name. Big deal," she added with more bravado than she felt.

"Would you want your brothers to know where you live? Would you want the men who worked for your father or the ones who worked against him to call you Jennifer and visit your classroom?"

"It...it depends."

The agent across from her scribbled in his notebook. Angel tried to read what he was writing, but it was upside-down and utterly illegible.

"It depends on whether you believe your father was a criminal," O'Malley said lazily. "And if you believe your brothers are equally guilty."

"My father was a building contractor," Angel said. "He built office buildings and shopping malls. When I left ten years ago, my brother Tony had just gotten into the carpenter's union and Rocco was an electrician's apprentice. Salvatore hoped to become an architect. His drawings of buildings are first-rate."

"Salvatore is very artistic," O'Malley agreed. "Sometimes I think he'd be happier as a starving artist in a garret. But all your brothers worked for your father. In construction. They say."

"Yes."

"Was he clean all those years?"

"He was never convicted. You indicted him three times on bribery, money laundering and squeezing protection money from small businesses. But nothing ever stuck, did it? So he must have been clean."

"Not guilty is different from innocent."

Angel looked out of the smoked-glass windows at the voluptuous oak trees that lined Green Bay Road. She tried to forget that she had, just a half hour before, thought of that same logic when talking to Tony.

"You wouldn't have left if you thought he was

legit," O'Malley said, leaning back and studying her carefully. "And you would have gone to the house to be with your brothers in their hour of grief if you had any faith that they were clean, too."

"What do you want from me?"

"I want help in nailing your parents' killer," O'Malley said. "They were gunned down outside that restaurant as if they were dogs. Your mother took eight shots altogether and your father took twelve. Your brother Rocco passed out when he was IDing the bodies at the morgue. Your father didn't have a face. Rocco had to look for a scar on his finger."

"But I would think the police would take care of this," she said, swallowing her horror at the grisly details.

"The police will be working under my office. We're treating this as being related to your father's criminal activities."

"And my mother?"

"An innocent. A true innocent. In the wrong place at the wrong time."

"So where do I fit in?"

"I think we want things from each other," O'Malley said, taking her soft, unlined hand in his own gnarled fingers. "You want to return to your life. I want to close up this investigation and clean up a little portion of the city. We both want killers in jail and our streets to be safe. I don't have any children, was never blessed with marriage, but if I did I wouldn't want their safety any more intensely than I want safety for all the children right now. The Sciopelli and Martin companies both hide businesses that do dirt and put danger on the streets."

"I'm not part of it."

"You can get in the house."

"My house?" Angel recoiled.

"The Sciopelli house. Your brothers still live at home, on the family compound. We want an insider there. And I think your brothers may have been involved in the killing."

Angel shook her head.

"I can believe a lot of things about my brothers, but that they would kill our parents is out of the question."

"Still, it would be a good thing to prove them innocent...or guilty," O'Malley countered. "It might even put your heart at ease, once and for all."

"I wouldn't think you'd care who killed my father."

"No, that's not true. Even though I think your father did many, many terrible things, I still believe he didn't deserve to be killed or to have his wife killed beside him. And furthermore, as an officer of the court, I am sworn to find his killer."

"I'm not looking for vengeance."

"But, Angel, doing the right thing is very different from running away."

She leaned forward, reaching past the anonymous assistant to tap on the glass partition separating her from the driver.

"Excuse me. Please stop the car now."

No response.

"Excuse me." She knocked more frantically on the smoke glass. "Excuse me, I want to get out of the car. Now."

The glass slid down. She looked back to see O'Malley's finger at the control for the window. She felt vaguely humiliated that she had had to rely on him, but she wasn't going to give another inch.

"Stop the car," she ordered.

The driver glanced back at his boss.

"Do it," O'Malley concurred.

"Thank you," she said as the car slid to a stop in front of a row of quaint Tudor-style shops.

"Before you go," O'Malley said, "I want you to consider something. You're a preschool teacher, right?"

"You know all about me."

"In Davenport, they don't have a lot of drugs. Not much prostitution. Not much illegal gambling. Am I right?"

"Yes, that's true."

"Chicago's a little different. It's a rough-and-tumble town that tries so hard to be civilized. But there's drugs. In the schools, even. Prostitution and drugs, illegal weapons sales. Your average preschool teacher in the Chicago public schools has already seen the fallout. It's bad, but the most terrifying part is that Chicago now is what Davenport will be in ten years. Your children will not be spared.''

''O'Malley, your office has spent a lot of resources targeting my family,'' Angel said, mimicking the rationale she knew her father would use. ''Three acquittals. Don't you think you should pick another target?''

''No.''

''Why not? You seem to have such a personal thing going.''

''Oh, Angel, it's always personal.''

''I'm going,'' she said.

''Fine,'' O'Malley said, directing the agent sitting in the jump seat to open the door for her. ''I'll make sure this gets to the right people. Tony's never seen your apartment. And Rocco would get such a kick out of visiting your classroom. Zach would want to come see you, wouldn't he?''

She paused, one foot on the curb, the other still in the car. O'Malley held up the file. It was her life. Her own life, the one she had spent ten years making for herself.

"Angel, if you thought they were good men, you wouldn't be afraid. And, Angel," he added, leaning forward out the window, "you should be afraid. We all should be very afraid."

Chapter Three

Angel pulled the brass lion's head of the Sciopelli house and let it fall. The vibration of the heavy knocker echoed her heart's fearful rhythm. The taxicab glided down the flagstone driveway, taking with it her means of escape.

The house hadn't changed much. Built more suitably for mild Mediterranean climate than for Chicago's rugged extremes, its walls were bleached stucco, the roof terra-cotta; arched windows soared and the oak doors were intricately carved. The senior Sciopelli had added on to the house with each business success—an octagonal turret, flagstone paths, expert landscaping with ornate wrought-iron furniture and voluptuous blooms imported from Europe.

Angel ran her fingers across her envelope purse, feeling the outline of her lipstick, her hairbrush, the roll of mints, a camera no bigger than her thumb and the slim little tape recorder that O'Malley swore would pick up even the slightest sound in the study.

Isn't there a parable involving sheep being led to slaughter? Angel thought grimly, looking back over the sun-dappled lawn of her childhood home.

The grass was green and shorn to a luxurious but neat three inches. The first summer cicadas buzzed ominously. Red poppies and white hostas waved gaily from the border on the street.

Angel reached for the scowling lion's head again.

Surely they would be home. It was a scant two hours since the service and although she would have missed most, if not all, of the people who came back to the house for refreshments, she was sure that the Sciopelli brothers didn't have anyplace else to go.

Still, the fact that they didn't open the door was ominous.

Maybe this wasn't going to work out after all, Angel thought, giving in to her queasiness.

Suddenly the heavy oak door swung open.

And Angel thought it might swing right back in her face because Maria looked blankly at her before her scowl was replaced with a joyful smile.

"Oh, my sister!" Maria shrieked. Quickly wiping her flour-dusted hands on an apron over her black mourning dress, she threw her arms around Angel. Angel struggled to maintain her breath and her balance. Holding tight, Maria screamed louder.

"Come quick! It's Angel! I almost didn't recognize her! She's come home—Tony, Tony, it's just like you hoped!"

Within seconds Tony, Rocco and Salvatore were crowding around Angel.

"Come in, come in, come in," Salvatore said shyly. He pushed forward a tall young waif dressed in a black shift that on any other woman would have looked like a bag. On this woman, it looked like haute couture. "Isabel, you remember Angel. You just met. My sister's been away for a while."

"I didn't even know you had a sister until today," Isabel said in a smooth-as-silk voice.

"Yeah, but she's back, right?"

"Nice to meet you again, Angel," Isabel said in a voice barely above a whisper. She held out a perfectly manicured hand. "Salvatore hasn't told me a thing about you."

"Isabel's a model," Salvatore said. "We met at the Martins' Christmas party—she was in for a showing of Kanae clothes. We're engaged."

"Salvatore, I'm sure she doesn't want to hear the history of our courtship while standing on the hot porch," Isabel chided, running her hand along his shoulder. "We'll have plenty of time to get acquainted."

Angel was quickly ushered into the house.

"Congratulations on your engagement," Angel

said just as Isabel stepped back against Salvatore to form a picture-perfect pose.

What could he be thinking of, marrying so young?

But then Angel realized that Salvatore must be twenty-six years old, one year younger than herself. That wasn't too young. Where had all the years gone?

Tony urged her into the cool foyer and closed the door behind her.

"So...you gonna stay for dinner?" Rocco asked gruffly. "Most of the guests have gone home already. We were gonna sit down and eat. I'm starvin'."

"Rocco, don't be pushy," Maria warned, and she added in a conciliatory voice, "Give Angel a chance to catch her breath. I hope you stay, Angel, but if you have to leave, we'll understand. Won't we, Tony?"

Tony gazed at Angel thoughtfully, clipping his white shirt cuffs to show an inch of linen with a white-on-white three-letter monogram.

"Zach said that he dropped you off at the train station because you didn't want to come here," he said calmly.

"I changed my mind," Angel replied.

"Wonderful," Tony said, his sole expression of emotion being the slight lift of his eyebrows. "Can you stay?"

"For dinner?"

"For dinner, yes. But why don't you make it longer?"

Things were going even better than O'Malley said they would! Angel thought to herself.

"Tony, don't pressure her," Maria said. "We don't even know why she's here."

"I just...just wanted to be with family."

"That's nice," Maria said.

"So she will stay for a week. At least," Tony insisted. "Maria, fix up the guest suite for her."

"Our housekeeper's at the Martins' house. She'll be coming back after dinner," Maria said. "I'll take care of it then. Do you have any bags with you?"

"No. They're at the hotel. Tony, Maria, I appreciate your hospitality."

"Please say you will stay with us," Tony said. "We can send to the hotel for your things."

"Of course I will, but I don't want to impose."

"Angel, this has been such a terrible time for us," Tony said. His voice rose as he addressed all the family standing in the marble-tiled foyer. "We need to come together, forget past problems, forgive one another. Because, Angel, family is all you really have in life."

"Yes," murmured Guy, Jr., who slipped behind Tony to put a hand on his shoulder. "Family is everything."

Tony shot him a disapproving glance. Jeanne Martin, looking very tired but still put together with exquisite taste, entered the foyer. She started when she saw Angel. Her scarlet-stained lips parted slightly and she took a steadying breath.

"My darling Angel, it's so wonderful you have come to the house," she said, recovering quickly. "Zach will be so happy to see you."

"What will Zach be happy about?" a voice behind Mrs. Martin said.

Tugging his tie, Zach walked out into the cool foyer, glanced around the gathering and did a double take when he saw Angel. He gave her an arrogant and provocative once-over.

"So, Angel, you must have changed your mind after I dropped you off," he said with unmistakable suspicion.

She caught her breath.

"I did," she said.

"You seemed so definite about leaving."

"I changed my mind."

"Did you walk here?"

"Took a cab."

"How'd you get a cab?"

"There was one at the station," she lied. O'Malley had had one waiting for the limousine when they had completed their talk.

"At this hour? On a Saturday? Lucky woman."

"Yes, I was very lucky," Angel insisted. Was it

her imagination or was everyone in the foyer calculating the odds of getting a cab at the Hubbard Woods station house? Zach stared at her from beneath half-closed lids.

"Luck is a very wonderful thing," Tony said, his words slicing into the uncomfortable silence. "We are lucky and glad you have come back. And we want you to stay. This is your home. The ten long years are over. Angel, welcome back."

Angel shivered, though the brilliance of the foyer's cathedral skylight was temperate.

"Dad, look who's here!" Guy exclaimed, waving his martini glass toward the Venetian doors leading to the courtyard. "Little Angel has returned."

Wheezing, his father struggled into the foyer.

"Oh, Angel, it's wonderful to see you," Guy, Sr., said. "Your father and mother would be so happy to know you are here. Come, come give me a kiss."

Angel walked unsteadily toward the man who was her godfather and would have been her father-in-law, well aware of the intensity of Zach's regard as she stepped past him. She kissed Guy, Sr.'s cheek, now wet with tears.

The old man pulled a handkerchief out of his suit jacket pocket and apologized, between coughs, for his lung cancer.

Angel patted his back reassuringly until he calmed. She hazarded a glance at Zach.

"Yes, it's a wonderful thing," Zach said, leaning

over to give her a perfunctory peck on the cheek. "I'm glad you changed your mind and came home."

"I had better check on dinner," Maria said.

Angel silently submitted to the tide of hospitality.

As the parade of family members came into the kitchen, Maria had glasses of wine and a platter of antipasto meats ready. She hugged Angel a second and then a third time. Tony squeezed Angel's shoulder, told her that he was sure she would understand that he had some business to conclude upstairs in the study.

"When you're done visiting, come up and see the shopping mall," he said proudly. "Salvatore designed the building, I put it into work and—"

"And I designed the interior," Maria interjected, pulling a casserole dish from the oven.

"She did. It's very much a family project."

"I'd be delighted to see it," Angel said.

Tony strode away.

"Here, let me take your purse," Maria said as Angel juggled a plate and a glass of wine. "I'll put it upstairs in the guest suite. I'll have the housekeeper put fresh sheets on the bed when she returns and we'll call your hotel and have your bags sent here."

"No, please, that's all right. I need my purse," Angel said abruptly, putting her glass and plate on the kitchen counter. "I...I wanted to freshen up."

"Sure," Maria said, stepping away. "I understand. The long day."

But the tone of her voice made it clear that she didn't understand the sudden determined tone of Angel's voice.

"Yes, the long day, that's it," Angel said, grasping at the excuse.

She slipped into the powder room and spilled the contents of her purse out onto the marble counter.

She thanked God that she had locked her wallet at the train station near the hotel. Nothing she carried identified her as Jennifer Smith. When this was over, she hoped she'd have the option of returning to Iowa.

She put the camera and small tape recorder into the pocket of her dress and scooped everything else back into her purse.

She flushed the toilet, ran the water for a few moments, crumpled a guest towel and came out into the hallway to bump right into Zach.

His jaw rippled with anger, and when he put his arm against the wall to block her path back to the kitchen, she felt afraid. Truly afraid.

"O'Malley got to you, didn't he?"

She swallowed air that felt as hot as fire.

"I...I don't know what you mean."

"You're no good at lying," Zach said. "That's why you should get out now before you have to learn or fail at it. Now, where is it?"

He grabbed her purse, flipping it open.

"Give me back my..." she demanded, careful to keep her voice down.

"How'd he persuade you? Did he tell you the fate of the innocent children of Chicago was in your hands?" He pawed through her purse and checked the lipstick to make sure it was. "He's good at using children—he can capture the right sense of remorse about never having had his own."

"He did say something about children."

"Did he weep? He can cry on demand, did you know that? Really good at turning on the emotion. I admire the man, even like him, but I know his faults and his weaknesses. He's using you, Angel."

"He's not! He's a very nice man," Angel told Zach, knowing full well O'Malley had her over a barrel.

"And how would you know?" Zach asked. His smile was long on triumph, but short on mirth.

"I'm not saying I do," Angel backtracked.

"Give me the recorder and the camera. I'm sure he gave you both. Along with a perfectly useless crash course in undercover work. Hand over."

"Zach, no, I—"

"Who did he say was going to pick up tapes and film? Who's the courier? Or did he ask you to go downtown every day for a confab at his office?"

"He didn't say." Angel felt off balance by Zach's questions. "I mean, I don't know what you're talking about."

"Are you sure?"

He shoved the purse back into her hands and then

ran a quick commanding caress over her hips. She was momentarily distracted from her irritation by the burst of sensation he awakened with his touch, but she recovered...just as he pulled the thin chain out from under the neckline of her dress.

In his broad, tanned hand, the gold ring with the small, square-cut peridot, her birthstone, and citrine, his birthstone, looked fragile—though it had survived ten years of wearing and not just a few flings across a lonely bedroom in her apartment.

He stared at the ring dangling from its chain and then closed it gently in his fist.

Angel knew he could see her vulnerability to him, her ten-year-long losing battle to forget him, and she tugged the ring out from his grasp and shoved it back under her dress collar with a suitably indignant look.

He didn't crumble.

"I can't protect you if you stay."

She wanted to ask him what he meant, but at that moment Maria called out from the kitchen.

"Angel, what hotel are you staying at? Tony says his foreman, Jimmy, lives downtown. He can go pick up your suitcases and check out for you."

"I'll go get them," Zach called out, running a flat palm down the back of Angel's dress. "I can pick them up after dinner."

"Tony says it'll be easier this way," Maria persisted. "You know how he gets when he's got an idea in his head. He says he wants to have a relaxing family dinner. No distractions.''

"What have you got at your hotel?'' Zach whispered, his icy mint breath gone hot against the base of her neck. "Think fast. Do you have anything there that could hurt you?''

"No,'' Angel said, remembering that any identification for Jennifer Smith was in the locker at the train station.

She had thought she was being overly careful when she rented the locker, but now she realized she had been right.

"Just a change of clothes.''

"Your plane ticket?''

"It's not there,'' she said cautiously. "I didn't want anyone to know my destination.''

"Good girl. You've grown some smarts.''

She nearly corrected him on several points, starting with "girl'' and ending with "smarts,'' but Maria called out again.

"I agree with Tony. I don't see what the problem is with sending Jimmy,'' Maria said. She slammed the oven door shut. "He lives downtown and it'd be too much trouble for you to...''

Maria turned the corner into the narrow hallway to the bathroom just as Zach wrapped a strong arm around Angel's waist and abruptly kissed her.

Chapter Four

His mouth was hard, his lips unrepentant, his head forcing hers back until she accepted his tongue like a sweet offering. Angel could only keep her balance by submitting to the strong, broad hand pressing at her lower back. The same hand that quickly made a sweep of her dress. Angel felt the camera and recorder slipping from the hip pocket of her dress into his fingers.

"Oh, you two are like a couple of kids," Maria cooed at the door to the kitchen. "Can't keep your hands off of each other, huh?"

Zach looked at her with a smile that was one part rogue and one part boyish charm.

"Caught me, didn't you?"

Maria shook her head, snapped a dish towel at him as if she were chastising a mischievous imp and went back to the kitchen.

"You two are so romantic." She sighed.

Angel glared at Zach, feeling unaccountably resentful of the kiss—and of the effect the kiss had upon her. She would not react to him, she ordered herself. He stood tall and took his hand out from behind her head. His triumphant smile transformed into a scowl.

He held up the camera and recorder.

"I can explain," Angel said, uncertain how she would, not having any clue as to his loyalties.

"Don't. I know how O'Malley operates. I can probably quote you everything he said to persuade you to do this. It's the stupidest thing you've ever done."

"Oh, really? I think the stupidest thing I've ever done was waiting for two days in the Las Vegas airport, thinking you were on your way."

Actually, the stupidest thing might be admitting the stupidest thing, Angel thought immediately after the words left her mouth.

She was a firm believer in personal dignity, in hiding her sorrows, in self-reliance and never giving herself a pity party. She was so appalled at her own outburst, she nearly missed his response.

He looked as if he might say something.

And then, lightning quick, his features hardened.

He slipped the recorder and camera into the inside pocket of his suit jacket.

"Get out, Angel, before it's too late," he warned.

He held her chin tight so that she couldn't look away. "And don't put your trust in Patrick O'Malley. The man talks big, but he's got his own agenda and it doesn't include saving your life. And if you stay in this house, I promise you your life will need saving."

He started to walk away, but she put her hand out to the opposite wall to block his path.

"If I'm going, shouldn't you give me a kiss goodbye?"

She blinked at him, her lips parted.

And he did. This time she responded to him as aggressively as an animal in heat. She put her hands into his jacket, feeling the taut ladder of muscles from his abdomen to his shoulders. She pressed one thigh against his maleness. For a selfish moment, she was glad he was still as affected by her as he had been as a younger man.

He shoved her away abruptly.

"This is goodbye, Angel," he said. "It has to be goodbye."

He held up her hotel key, which had been jangling at the bottom of her purse. Sauntering into the kitchen without a backward glance, he called out to Maria that he would personally drive Angel downtown after dinner to her hotel.

"If you want some time alone, don't go to her hotel room," Maria suggested. "Tony will have a fit. He's very old-fashioned, you know. Isabel and Salvatore have to sleep in separate bedrooms and they're engaged.''

"I'll keep that in mind," Zach said, and walked out to the living room.

Angel stood in the hallway between the powder room and the kitchen. Her hair felt tousled, and as she rubbed the back of her hand against the remnants of his kiss, she saw that her pale lipstick had been smudged into disrepair. Her heart was galloping, her legs were wobbly and her lower belly had become furnace hot.

She rued her lack of experience with the opposite sex that made her so vulnerable to Zach. But his desire for her left him vulnerable, too. She opened her hand to the camera and recorder she had liberated from his suit jacket pocket before replacing them in her pocket.

She took a couple of deep breaths and walked into the kitchen and told Maria that she'd be delighted to help with dinner.

"No, no," Maria said. "Rocco, please get her out of here. Her first day home and we're putting her to work? No way!"

Rocco, who had been lingering near the antipasto tray, grunted and led her upstairs to the study. Tony, his shirtsleeves rolled up and his tie askew, sprang to his feet from his place at her father's desk. Salvatore and Guy, Jr., looked up from their chairs on the other side of the desk.

It was clear the men had been involved in an intense conversation, one that had left Guy, Jr., red faced and Salvatore somber.

"Come on in, Angel," Tony said, gesturing to the tiger maple conference table by the fireplace. "See our magnificent shopping mall."

"All right."

"Winnetka has been such a small suburb, nearly choking on its own tax base," Tony said, warming to the topic. "But with the revenue generated by the shopping mall, the town will be able to afford to build a new elementary school, put in an enhanced 911 system and expand the park district summer programs."

The scale model was impressive, made lifelike with cut-glass archways and clay trees. Salvatore, obviously proud, explained he had built the model from balsa wood and other materials.

"I designed the mall," he admitted, unrolling the impressive blueprints. "But the real work will be in building it, of course. Drawing is just, well, using a pencil and paper."

The deference to Tony and Rocco started another conversation about the troubles facing a contractor. Rocco complained vociferously about zoning regulations and the building inspector. While he did, Angel backed up against the bookshelf.

"I'm just doing the grunt work," Guy, Jr., said, leaning unsteadily on the arm of his chair. "The hauling, the lifting, the trucking, the demolition. They wouldn't trust me with the important things."

"That's because you can't be trusted," Rocco retorted.

Angel used the momentary distraction to shove the recorder in the space between two books. With her index finger, she checked to make sure the voice activator button was flipped on.

"Gentlemen, gentlemen," Tony said. "This isn't a business meeting. This is merely an opportunity to show Angel what we're working on."

He looked at Angel with some scrutiny, but she stepped away from the bookshelf and kept her face as blank as possible.

Aiming for that I'm-just-a-girl-who-can't-understand-business-talk look.

"But, Tony, we got issues to work out," Guy, Jr., insisted. "I got workers to pay."

Pointedly ignoring Guy, Jr., Tony retrieved his suit jacket from the arm of his desk chair.

"I believe I hear Maria calling," he said, slipping on his jacket and shooting his cuffs. "She's made a marvelous dinner. Let's not keep her waiting."

And he left the study without a backward glance.

"We got to get this settled," Guy muttered, but Rocco and Salvatore were escorting Angel downstairs, working to fill the uncomfortable silence with talk of Salvatore's next project—a new chapel for the cathedral.

Downstairs, Maria insisted that Angel take the seat at Tony's right side. Angel agreed, grateful to put some distance between herself and Zach, who helped his father into a seat at the far end of the table.

But then he walked right back to her and leaned down to give her a kiss on the back of her neck.

"Where did you put it?" he murmured.

So he had figured out that she had taken the tape recorder and camera right back from him!

"Zach, you sit down with your father," Tony said, tugging at his sleeve.

Zach retreated, but a glance to Angel let her know that there'd have to be a confrontation after dinner.

She didn't look forward to that.

But a Sciopelli family dinner was no place for solitary thoughts. Just as she remembered from her childhood, the table was a bazaar of interlocking conversations, excited interruptions, sudden outbursts of laughter and raised glasses.

Although Tony opened with a few somber words about the tragedy they had endured, Isabel was the only one who did not try her best to fulfill his admonition that his parents had always wanted mealtimes to be pleasurable. Salvatore encouraged her to eat, but she relentlessly pushed her food around her plate with her fork and complained that she felt just heartsick about the tragedy that had befallen the Sciopellis.

But Tony and Maria pointedly played good hosts and drew their guests into light conversation.

"So," Maria said firmly as she seated herself across from Angel after bringing in the pasta course. "Does this mean that you and Zach are going to get back together again? I've heard that renewed first love affairs are the most intense."

"Where'd you hear that?" Tony asked, interrupting his own explanation to Rocco that he alone could choose the most delicious eggplant roll filled with chicken and vegetables that would be good enough for Angel.

"Tony, it was in one of those women's magazines," Maria replied.

Angel hazarded a glance down at the other end of the table. Guy, Jr., held his weight up with his elbows, leaning across the table to share with Rocco an incident in which Guy had bested one of his subcontractors. Rocco stared uncomfortably at his plate.

When Guy sat back at the satisfied conclusion of his tale, Angel had a clear picture of Zach.

He was cutting his father's meat for him, but as if

sensing Angel's gaze, he looked up. Meeting her eyes and then glancing at Tony.

"So what do you think, Angel?" Tony asked. "Are we finally going to throw rice and hear wedding bells for you and Zach?"

She blinked at her brother.

"I think it's way too early to talk like that," she said with what she hoped was perfect diplomacy.

"Angel, you've known him all your life," Maria reminded. "You were betrothed to him by your father on the day of your baptism. I was there—remember, Rocco and I were in nursery school together!"

"The promise was just meant as a joke," Angel said.

"Seems like everyone took the joke very seriously," Isabel offered, reluctantly taking a tiny bite of pasta at Salvatore's urging.

"Especially Zach," Tony said.

Not seriously enough, she thought to herself.

With poignant bravado, Salvatore popped the cork on a bottle of the very best Perrier-Jouët champagne from the cellar and the long table of family toasted her return. Tony tried very hard to keep the tone of the meal light and happy, recounting anecdotes about childhood that kept everyone smiling.

As a dessert of cannoli and fruit came to a close and the tiring, eventful day caught up with everyone, a more somber mood prevailed and soon everyone was imitating Isabel's restless grief.

Rocco abruptly stood and sang a favorite lullaby their mother had used to soothe all four children.

While everyone praised his talent, there were damp eyes as people remembered Mrs. Sciopelli.

"Do Darth Vader," Salvatore suggested. "It's Isabel's favorite."

Isabel looked up sullenly from her plate.

"I prefer Stallone."

"No, do Arnold Schwarzenegger," Jeanne Martin countered. "'I'll be back,' he says."

"Rocco, do Mrs. Tobin," Maria said. She leaned across the table to explain to Angel. "We have a housekeeper who comes in on the days when I go into the office. I told you I'm doing the interior design for the Winnetka Shopping Mall, didn't I? Well, Rocco does the most wicked imitation of our housekeeper. He's really very talented. Isn't he, Tony?"

"Yes, Maria."

Rocco held up his hand to silence the chorus of requests.

"I will not do Mrs. Tobin, because that would be cruel," he said to Maria. "Instead, I shall do one just for Angel."

He composed himself and, as he did so, a subtle reorganization of his features took place. He spoke in a subtle Southern drawl.

"Eight years ago, I was called upon to serve—"

"The president! The president!" shrieked Isabel, for the first time showing some emotion. "That's the president of your country."

"Yours, too," Salvatore said. "As soon as we get married."

Rocco acknowledged the table's burst of applause with a regal bow.

"You're just as great as always," Angel said.

"I can do one better," Guy, Jr., said, rising unsteadily to his feet. "It is a man who's been a real pain in the—"

"Just do it, Guy," Tony interrupted, his courteous demeanor strained to its breaking point.

The room quieted, anticipating. Guy squared his shoulders, drew his eyebrows down and lifted one side of his mouth in a sneer.

"I told you the first day you walked into this office, Zachary Martin, that one day you'd have to choose. And today is that day."

O'Malley's voice, with a rendition that was so eerily perfect that, for a scant moment, Angel thought O'Malley himself had slipped into the room. She looked at Zach, but he avoided her gaze.

The silence at the table grew oppressive, infecting everyone with sullen lethargy. Guy, Jr., smiled out the side of his mouth, getting some kind of pleasure from the uncomfortableness of his audience.

"Siddown, Guy," his father said.

His mother abruptly announced she had to phone the house and check on Anna.

"Guy, that wasn't nice," Maria said as Mrs. Martin left the room. "It's been a difficult situation for Zach."

"But it was a good imitation," Zach admitted. "It was right on target."

"Uncanny, actually," Tony said.

"Really?" Angel challenged coolly.

"Yeah," Zach said. "Do you recognize the voice?"

Angel felt her face go hot as everyone looked at her.

"No," she lied. "I don't. Who is it?"

Chapter Five

"That's Zach's boss, Patrick O'Malley," Tony explained. "The state's attorney who nearly drove father to an early grave. I don't think I've ever heard someone capture his voice quite like that."

He stopped, his face drawn and pale. He stared directly at Guy, Jr., with contemptuous wonder. Crumpling under his glare, Guy, Jr., muttered an apology.

"No, no, Guy, you just did a good job, that's all," Tony said. "It just was so perfect, so on target. Wasn't it, Zach?"

"Zach, you work for O'Malley?" Angel asked.

The room grew still. Everyone stared at Zach.

He leaned back in his chair.

"I don't exactly work for him," he replied. "I do appellate work. I write the legal briefs to support the verdicts juries come to. He wins a case, I defend to the higher court what he did."

"Good thing he's never had to write a brief explaining a guilty verdict for your father, right, Tony?" Guy asked, desperately trying to regain some kind of camaraderie.

Tony's chilly expression drove Guy to pour himself another drink and slump a little lower in his chair.

"Did he ever ask you to choose?" Angel asked.

Maria stifled a cough.

"Yes," he said, two hard gray eyes never leaving Angel's face.

"And did you?"

"He must have chosen if he's here," Guy, Sr., said, struggling to put an end to the conversation. "And he chose his family above some two-bit politician who's trying to make a name for...himself by persecuting a couple of family-owned...bus-businesses. He chose his family and...and...and..."

Zach's father's labored breathing became a cough and his cough wouldn't stop. Guy handed him a glass of water. Isabel offered a napkin. Salvatore said the oxygen tank was in the living room and he and Zach helped Mr. Martin out of the room.

Eerily calm, Tony took Angel's hand in his and whispered confidentially.

"I hope you don't think we blame you for leaving. When the first indictment came in, it must have been hard not to believe Father was some kind of monster.

But he wasn't a bad man. He was just a businessman trying to make a living.''

Angel saw a chance to stop the madness once and for all.

"Who killed him?"

Tony stared at her reproachfully.

"The police have no leads. It could have been anyone," he said, shrugging. "I hope they catch whoever did this, but I am resigned to the fact that the criminal justice system will not bring our parents back to us. And that's really all that matters to me. I'm not about vengeance, Angel."

Tears filled his eyes.

He blinked and looked away.

Angel squeezed his hand, feeling the love for her brother that had been so muted and confused for the past ten years.

"Is that why you're here, Angel, to find their killers?" Tony asked. "Because the murderer isn't in this house."

"No, no, I'm here because—"

"She's here because ten years is a long time to be away from your family," Zach said, returning to the dining room. "And we don't want her to feel unwelcome, do we, Tony?"

"No, of course not," Tony agreed. He pushed his chair away from the table. "Has your father recovered from his attack?"

"He's resting in the downstairs guest room," Zach said. "He needs a good half hour with his oxygen tank and then I think he'll be strong enough that we can drive him home."

"He can stay overnight."

"No, he insists on being in his own bed. Why don't I drive Angel down to her hotel to pick up her bags? My brother says you have some business to talk over in the study and you know how I feel about business."

"Bored. Ah, the life of a carefree playboy," Tony quipped. He stood. "But you don't need to drive all that way." Tony addressed Angel then. "Jimmy brought back your bags and I'll have them sent to your room."

"I thought I was driving her back to her hotel," Zach said.

"Ah, you are too hasty in your courtship," Tony replied. "You don't go driving off into the night with my sister without announcing your intentions."

And he strode out of the dining room without a backward glance. Guy, Jr., Rocco and Salvatore followed. Isabel shoved her chair back, said she was tired and went upstairs. Maria said to leave the plates because Mrs. Tobin would take care of them. She followed Isabel upstairs.

"Then we'll go for a walk in the garden," Zach said.

"Actually, I have other plans," Angel said. "I think I'll spend some time in my room."

With lightning speed reflexes, he grabbed her wrist and brought her to her feet.

"No, Angel, you really want to go for a walk," he said, his voice low. "That is, if you value your life half as much as I do."

Rather than resist, she followed him out onto the courtyard, past the flowers and to the pool. The vegetation was overgrown, several tiles on the surround were missing, but otherwise everything was exactly as it had been ten years before.

"You're leaving," Zach said. "I'm going to put you in a cab and I'm going to do everything in my power to make sure that no one goes after you."

"Why?"

"Because they're tearing apart the study."

"No, they aren't," she said.

"Yes, they are. You took the camera and the recorder back from me, didn't you?"

"Yes, I did," she said defiantly. "Are you my courier or not?"

"There isn't going to be a courier. As soon as I get my hands on O'Malley, I'll—"

"Make him send me home?"

"You'll already be home," he said darkly. "Because I'm telling you to go home."

Angel wagged a finger at him.

"Make sure you pick up the recorder."

"The recorder is in the study?"

"Yes."

"Oh, no. And the camera?"

"Someplace safe. I'll see if I can take pictures of documents some other time."

"They'll find the recorder tonight and shake you down for the camera. Now you know you can't stay."

She sighed in exasperation. "They're talking to your brother about something to do with the shopping mall."

"Let's just get you on a plane out of here."

She pointedly sat down on the concrete bench.

"You sure like to get me out of town."

"Is that a comment about ten years ago?"

"Take it any way you want. Are you working for O'Malley or not?"

"I work in the same office. I talk to the man about cases. But I don't report to him. And I'm not working for him now."

"Why didn't you tell me that—when you kissed me?"

"Because it doesn't matter who I work for. I never do anything for him that would affect the Sciopelli or Martin families. And I don't want you working for him."

"It's none of your business what I do."

"It is if it's going to get you killed."

"And how would that happen if you were doing your job and helping me?"

"No, that's not my job."

"How can you work in that office if you don't believe in the law?"

"I do believe in the law. Aw, Angel, what I'm doing now shouldn't interest you."

"You're right. It shouldn't. We aren't married, we aren't engaged, we aren't betrothed anymore. I'm a free woman and I can do what I want."

He slumped down beside her, pulling his tie free and shoving it into his pocket.

"Look, I never meant to hurt you—"

"This isn't about then," she snapped.

"It is, too."

"No, it isn't," she replied, annoyed at his arrogance. "I admit it—I sat in the Las Vegas airport watching at the gate of every incoming Chicago flight. It took me two days to figure out you weren't coming. I waited for you, then took the flight just like you said. That hurt. But it's over. Ten years is a long time. I've made another life for myself. And I intend on going back to it. After I'm finished here."

In ten years he had played out in his mind what she would say, what he would say, if they ever met. He had never been able to explain to her why he had stayed, and he found he couldn't do it now, either.

He couldn't explain the horrible choice that had confronted him—all he could tell her was that he had known, had been comforted by the knowledge that she was strong, stronger than the people who relied on him to stay. And that, in a subtle but unmistakable way, his remaining at home had been her surest protection.

"I'm sorry," he said simply. And then saw his duty—a kindness that would have to be cruel. "We were kids, I was immature—didn't know what I wanted."

Her revulsion was as palpable as it was quickly replaced with a shaken head. The gesture, one nearly of pity, touched him more deeply than pure anger would have.

The scent of chlorine and roses mingled in the air, and he was brought back to ten years before. When he had first discovered that his role as guardian protector would only be fulfilled if he sent her away. And if he stayed behind.

He thought he had made peace with his life. He didn't realize how much it clawed at him until she touched his cheek, marveling at a tear that had slipped unbidden from his squeezed-shut eyes.

"No, that's not true," he said. "I knew exactly what I wanted. I wanted you."

"You did have me."

"But I didn't know you knew...about things."

"It was the end of my innocence."

"Yes, it was."

"This place is just like it was that night," Angel reminisced. The garden was magical, the mist of the pool an intoxicating ether; everything conspired to make her remember, to turn the pages of time back ten years.

He answered her implicit question with a nod. "It's the same," he said, and he glanced up at the lit window on the second floor. "And I still can't go with you. Please leave. Fly to Las Vegas and take a connecting flight to wherever you live. Somebody could be watching you, so don't go back directly. Cover your tracks well."

"You won't come with me?"

"No, I can't," he said.

She stood and intently looked at him before she backed up and, finally finding it within herself to turn around, walked away.

"Angel, I love you," he said. "I always have. I always will."

She stopped dead in her tracks. She wasn't sure she had heard him correctly, and she didn't have the nerve to ask him to repeat himself.

He strode behind her and touched her hair. She turned around.

"Damn you, I'm a fool to have loved you," she said. "I can't love another man, you know. It is as if you made me your wife and I feel like I'm cheating if I even look at another man. Isn't that crazy?''

"Not so crazy," he said, a dimpled smile letting her know that he understood, maybe even felt the same way. "But it doesn't change the facts."

"And what are the facts?"

"You have to leave, Angel," he said. "You'll be used as a pawn or worse by O'Malley or by your brothers, and you'll be in danger yourself."

"Did you really love me?"

"Always and forever."

"Do you love me now?"

"With every breath I take. But I still have to send you away. To protect you and to protect others."

"Others?"

"Don't ask. Just go."

"Why can't I stay?"

"Because if you stay, I can't stop myself from wanting you, from wanting you to be my wife. And if you are, then the Martin and Sciopelli families are joined. Think of the power that comes together. Think of the alliances that would be forged."

"We could avoid all that."

"No, we couldn't. Think of what our children would represent to people who would do wrong. Think of how they could be used."

In a moment of blinding clarity, she understood.

"We give them what they want by being together.

And we'd become something that we now cannot bear to consider. Get out of here, Angel.''

"I'm not a child anymore," she said. "I don't like being told what to do. You can't order me around like you used to."

"Did I order you around?"

"No, but I did everything that you told me to do. Just because I loved you so much."

"How about if I ask you to leave?"

She hesitated.

He glanced up at the second-story window. He bristled with sudden impatience.

"I wish I had a lifetime to give you," he said. "I wish I had at least a night to make love to you. But all I have to give you is a kiss goodbye," he said, and thinking he saw a flicker of movement in the second-floor study and not liking the thought of being watched, he picked her up and carried her to the cabana. He kicked the door, slamming it upon the Sciopelli family woes and laid his betrothed upon the chintz cushioned chaise.

"This is wrong," Angel whispered, even as her legs coiled around his.

"You're right. This is wrong."

But the feelings she had kept under wraps for so long overwhelmed any logic that would have propelled her out the door.

"Is it wrong?" she asked.

"No, this is right," he said, surrendering to the potent memory. "This is the first right thing I've done in a long time."

Chapter Six

He was sure of himself and his touch. Or maybe it was simply that she brought him back to a time when he was young and bold, when the cynicism and weight of responsibility didn't crush quite so hard.

Whether a male confidence intrinsic to himself or a return of youthful innocence swept in by her presence, he was a man of power and passion.

They made love a first time in great urgency, not even bothering to discard every article of clothing. He had waited, beyond hope, for ten years and could not wait a moment longer once she opened herself to him. When he entered her, she was white-hot and silky soft. And her face glowed radiant in the moonlight, her hair tumbling in seafoam waves on the chaise cushion.

As he moved against her, she looked at him, that same look of surprise at the moment of ecstasy that she had blessed him with—just once—ten years before.

And then her contractions did away with all his self-control. He came with her name on his lips.

The second lovemaking was more slow and deliberate, but also more tender and tragic. Both knew as they lingered in caress that this was a moment of memory, their fingers and lips would have to carry their love in separate hearts, separate lives.

Finally, it was ten minutes before they really should get back to the house. Then five minutes before their absence would be noted. Both feeling as if the sands of time were slipping through their entwined fingers.

As they lay on the chaise, they didn't speak, knowing that the only topic of conversation available was how they would soon be apart. Forever.

But even in this intimacy, Angel experienced a quiver of rebellion. What if she didn't do what Zach told her to do? What if she stayed? What if she persuaded him to help her? What if O'Malley could break the chain of crime and free them all? What if…?

And Zach lay wondering how he would distract and detain the brothers when they learned Angel had fled. When they learned that she had been used by O'Malley. When they turned their claws on Zach and forgot for a moment, as they no doubt would, the uneasy truce they had lived under while he worked in the same office as their father's most potent enemy.

Zach jerked his head up.

"What is it?" Angel asked.

"Noises. From the house. I can't tell if it's arguing or singing or—"

A single shotgun blast answered the question.

Zach leapt to his feet, struggling with his pearl-covered shirt buttons. He checked that his gun was in his shoulder holster. Angel scrambled behind him, tugging her linen dress down over her shoulders.

They sprinted past the pool—she was barefoot, carrying her pumps in her hand—down the marble steps of the garden path.

Zach nearly tripped over his father's wheelchair in the courtyard.

"What's going on?"

"Your brother took a shot at Rocco," his father snarled. "But he missed. A drunken argument about the shopping mall."

"Not again."

"Last time they used fists. It's getting worse. Dammit, Zach, marry her," he urged, shoving his oxygen mask onto his face. His next words were barely intelligible, but his point was clear. "Marry this Angel, make peace with this family, or we're all going to be destroyed."

He jerked a hand in Angel's direction. She stopped dead in her tracks. A terrible keening arose from the house. The two men looked at Angel.

"What did I do?" she asked.

Zach shook his head wearily.

"Get him out of here, Angel," he ordered. "Help him to my car out front. Here's the keys. Drive him home. I'm going inside."

He didn't wait for her assent.

Instead, he pulled his gun out of its shoulder holster and bolted for the house.

"Go on after him," Guy Martin, Sr., said, tugging his mask away. He wheezed miserably.

"He told me to—"

"No, Angel, do what you think is right. After all, it's your brothers, my son…and your future husband. I'm not going anywhere. Except if the good Lord asks me for a walk."

She hesitated. And then lit off after Zach. In the foyer, Rocco and Guy, Jr., grunting and cursing, were locked in a struggle for a gun. Blood from either or both men smeared the white marble floor as they rolled first one way and then another.

The gun went off a second time, a bullet ricocheting on a marble panel inlaid along the wall and blasting a crystal vase. Water, flowers and sparkling shards of glass spilled onto the two men.

Maria screamed and ran up the stairs, telling Tony

to stop them. Isabel leaned over the railing to watch, babbling in an excited mix of Spanish, Italian, French and English.

"Calm down, Isabel," Mrs. Martin said, giving up on her efforts at ordering Guy to stop fighting. "Maria, let's get her to her room. This poor girl's hysterical. She's probably never even seen a gun before."

Standing in the downstairs doorway, Salvatore hesitantly implored the two men to stop fighting and kept an eye on the women taking his fiancée down the upstairs hall.

"Tony, dammit, do something!" Maria shrieked. "Rocco's going to get hurt if you don't!"

Tony, standing at the foot of the bridal staircase, remained oddly transfixed by the violence, as if he were watching a particularly interesting television program. He did not even flinch when a third bullet was fired, shooting a pane out of the front door.

Zach stepped to the center of the foyer and, with no more effort than one might use to separate brawling children, yanked Guy to his feet and ordered Rocco to stand.

The gun clattered to the bloodstained floor as Rocco stumbled upright. Mindful of the broken glass, Angel put on her pumps. Then she slipped between the men, recovered the gun and backed off into the narrow maid's corridor leading to the kitchen.

"You all right?" Zach asked, steadying Rocco with an outstretched hand.

Rocco wiped his bloody mouth and nose with a handkerchief. Fresh blood spurted from his nostrils.

"Yeah, I guess," he muttered. "But your jackass brother started it."

Guy jockeyed for a resumption of the fight, but Tony stepped forward, reinforcing Zach's position.

"Settle down," Zach warned both men.

"All I want is what I'm entitled to," Guy shouted. He eyeballed Rocco. "Your father was fair to me and my family. I got a business to run, I got workers depending on me, and if I don't get treated fairly by you boys, there's going to be people who're going to pay. And it won't be me or my workers."

"Well, things are going to be different with us in charge," Rocco sputtered, stanching the blood that would not stop. He drew himself up with supreme dignity and peered over Zach's shoulder. "Things are very different now. You're talking to the bosses now."

"You won't cut me out!" Guy bellowed. He pushed past Tony and shoved Zach with his left hand, leaving a dark handprint on the bleached white shirt. Both men stared, momentarily distracted by the proof of Guy's injury. Zach flicked open Guy's suit jacket to assess the damage.

"Oh, my God," he muttered.

"It's a shoulder wound," Guy snarled, clearly peeved at his younger brother's ignorance. "It's not much. I'll recover. It would help if you took a little interest in your family's livelihood. Then I wouldn't have to fight these battles on my own."

"Actually, Guy, I don't think there are any battles you've ever fought on your own," Tony said.

Guy spit at him.

"You know, Guy, I've never liked you," Tony responded, brushing at the spittle on his lapel.

"I'm heartbroken. But let's get something straight, Tony. I won't be cut out, and frankly, I know so much about what's going on in your family that I could bring you all down to your knees."

"You really don't know all that much," Tony said calmly.

Rocco looked over at his brother, waiting for an instruction to charge. It never came.

Instead, Tony sighed, shrugging off his suit jacket.

"Maria, would you make sure Mrs. Tobin gets this to the dry cleaner?" he asked.

"Sure, Tony," Maria said, standing at the top of the stairs but not yet daring to come down to the foyer. Tony dropped the jacket on the floor.

"You bring a gun to my home on the night of my parents' funeral," he chided Guy. "You ask to speak about business. We accommodate you. We tell you we are dissatisfied with some of the work your people are doing on the Winnetka Shopping Mall project and that we want a credit.''

"You don't want a credit," Guy snarled. "You want to cut me out of the deal. Besides, that's not where the money comes from and you know it. It's what I haul when my trucks are empty that counts.''

He hazarded a glance at Angel, but she kept her face neutral.

"Get out of my house," Tony said calmly. "And don't come back.''

"Tony, no," Mrs. Martin said, from the top of the stairs. "Your parents would be so upset if they could see all of you now.''

"Actually, Mrs. Martin, I don't think my father would be so upset," Tony corrected. "Now, Guy, there's the door.''

"Watch your back, Tony," Guy replied, and he threw off Zach's arms.

"Guy, say you're sorry," Mrs. Martin pleaded.

"No way, Ma.''

Having seen enough, Angel charged into the foyer.

"Wait, Tony, Rocco, Guy, come on. Be reasonable. We're all really grief-stricken and shocked by our parents' murders. We're not thinking clearly. I'm sure if there's any kind of disagreement you have, you can resolve it in the morning, when everyone will be less on edge.''

"I'm leaving, little Miss Sunshine," Guy snapped.

"You don't waltz in after ten years and set everyone straight. You don't have a clue what's going on."

"I know you are reacting a little more emotionally than you should."

"Angel, it's not your fight," Zach said softly.

"Zach, I just want these guys to stop fighting."

Guy shook his head and jabbed a bloody finger toward Tony.

"If you want war, it's war you're going to get."

"Fine!" Rocco shouted. "We don't need your family anymore. It was just our father who kept us tied to your family. And he always gave you work even though you never deserved it."

Angel drew closer to Zach. As she did so, she was uncomfortably aware of Tony's silent scrutiny. He stared at her and then at Zach.

"Angel's right," Tony corrected his brother cautiously. "Perhaps we should stop fighting. Let's meet tomorrow morning. We'll talk business and resolve this little problem without any more bloodshed. Guy, get yourself to a doctor."

Guy muttered that he was fine.

"Do what I tell you. It's just a flesh wound, but still, somebody should see that thing."

"I'll take him to Evanston Hospital," Zach said. "Angel, take Ma and Dad home."

"No way, little brother," Guy said with as much dignity as he possessed. "The hospital will ask questions about how this happened. The police will be called in. I'm not that much of a fool."

"At least we agree on something," Tony said. "Take him over to my guy, Dr. Morgan. His house is on the corner of Locust and Elm. He's discreet—I'll call and tell him you're on your way. Rocco, do you need to go see Dr. Morgan, too?"

"Nah, I've just got a bloody nose," Rocco said, daintily dabbing his handkerchief at his nostrils. He looked over at Tony and then at Guy, Jr. "Sorry, Guy, lost my temper."

"Yeah, sorry," Guy said perfunctorily. "Tomorrow. We'll talk. Get this settled."

"So we're agreed," Tony said, bringing his palms together. "No fighting, no precipitous actions until we meet tomorrow morning. We can work this out. Angel's absolutely right—we're all on edge, we're not thinking straight. Right, Rocco?"

"But, Tony, you said...right, Tony. I mean, right, Angel."

Angel handed Zach his car keys, but he shook his head.

"I'll take Guy's car. You drive my father and mother home in mine. Wait there for me."

"You're not taking Angel away from us, are you?" Tony asked.

"No, of course not," Zach said. "I'll get her home later tonight."

"You'd better," Tony warned playfully. "After all, I'm her older brother and I set a very strict curfew."

Zach put a helping hand under Guy's elbow as they walked out onto the porch. Guy swatted him away with his good arm and Zach didn't push it.

Angel stood at the front door and watched the two brothers get into the car.

"Blessed be the peacemakers," their father said, wheeling up behind her, "for they shall inherit the earth."

"Mr. Martin, I hate to correct your quotation of the Bible, but I think it's the meek who will inherit the world."

"The meek never get anything." Mr. Martin snorted. "Especially not a chunk of the world."

Chapter Seven

"Mr. O'Malley, I hope it's not too late," Angel said quietly into the phone in the upstairs study of the Martin home. "But you told me I could call anytime I knew something or needed help."

"No, no, Angel," he said, clearly struggling to wake up. "What's up?"

"I'm leaving tonight."

"What?"

"I'm leaving. And I'm not coming back."

"You can't do that," O'Malley said coldly, quickly coming awake. "We have an agreement."

"I don't want to be part of it anymore."

"Did Zach tell you to leave?"

"As a matter of fact, he did. But—"

"Traitor."

"Look, leave him alone. He's doing the best he can."

"You're defending him. You must still have a thing for him."

"You should have told me that he worked for you."

"That's not strictly true. He's actually in the appellate division."

"Stop talking like a lawyer. He works in your office. He walks a tightrope for you."

"You two went out in high school, didn't you? Wasn't there something about your christening? Some ancient ritual where you were promised to him?"

"Don't play dumb. If you were smart enough to figure out the rest of my life you had to have figured this one out."

"Look, did you get anything?" O'Malley switched subjects.

"No, but there was a fight."

"A fight?"

"Rocco and Guy, Jr. They went up to the study after dinner to talk over some business matters and it got very contentious. The brawl spilled out into the rest of the house."

"Rocco and Guy? Is Guy all right?"

"They struggled with a gun and Guy got shot, but I think it seemed like it was probably a flesh wound because he was able to walk out of the house on his own," Angel said, before realizing that the question itself was surprising. "Why do you ask?"

"Just wondering," O'Malley said. "I figure any fight with Rocco and Guy is going to end with Rocco on top. He's quite a scrapper, that one. Real big guy. What hospital is Guy going to? And who's taking him?"

"Zach is with him. And they're going to some doctor that Tony recommended so that the police won't be called in. Do you want to hear the rest of this?"

"Yeah, sure. It's just I'm a detail guy. Want to know everything about everything before I hear the next thing. How's Rocco?"

"He's got a bloody nose. They're going to have a meeting at ten tomorrow. Something about the shopping mall project and how they feel that Guy is not doing a good job. Guy feels he's not being fairly treated."

"You have to stay."

"I'm leaving."

"No, Angel, think about the innocent people who live every day with the consequences of the criminal enterprise that's hidden within the legitimate family business," O'Malley said. "Hold on, I've got to turn on my light. Where was I? Oh, yeah. The prostitution, drugs, gambling, kickback schemes. It affects our children's futures."

"O'Malley, are you going to start crying now?" she asked, thinking of Zach's cynical observations of his co-worker's acting ability.

"I might. I sometimes get pretty worked up about criminals. Why do you ask?"

"Well, don't bother. I'm not so sure about you anymore."

"What's that supposed to mean?"

"It means I think you're using me."

"Of course I'm using you. I'm just using you for a good cause. You're not leaving Chicago," O'Malley said. "I've got a file on you. I know exactly who you are and where you are. And don't think of trying to make a break for some new town, changing your name again, because I'd just figure that one out, too. And if you take Zach... I swear you'll have me, your brothers and his family forming a posse to look for you. I'm your protection, Angel. Zach's protection, too."

"I thought you might do this," she said. "Zach warned me."

"I'm a jerk. But that's because I'm a prosecutor. What can I say?"

"All right, what do you want me to do?" she asked woodenly.

"Follow the instructions. Get into the study."

"I already did that."

"Did you take any pictures? Put the recorder in? Did you catch the argument?"

"No, I wasn't there for the argument. I got the recorder hidden in a bookshelf. I didn't have time to retrieve it."

"Well, make time in your busy schedule because this is important. That argument might have the key to the whole business. Take the camera and get pictures of any files and documents. Make sure there's a fresh tape in the recorder for the ten o'clock meeting. And give the tape and the film from the camera to Zach. He'll bring them to me."

"What if he doesn't cooperate with you?"

"He will—when it's your life he's saving. Oh, and Angel? Contact me as soon as you hear anything about Guy's condition. Rocco's, too."

He hung up.

Angel gently put the phone down.

"How's O'Malley?" a voice from behind her said.

Angel whirled around. Mrs. Martin, wearing the same beautiful silk suit she had worn to the funeral, stood in the doorway. How long had she been listening? Angel opened her mouth to protest that she hadn't been talking to O'Malley and then decided it was useless.

"He's fine."

"Still determined to get his way?" The question

was said without the hostility O'Malley usually engendered in the Martin and Sciopelli homes.

"Yeah," Angel said.

"Cantankerous, isn't he?"

"I suppose you could call him that. Do you know him personally?"

"I used to know him quite well," Mrs. Martin said. "But it's been more than thirty years."

"Really?"

"We all grew up in the same neighborhood. Your father, my husband, O'Malley, me, even your mother. In Bridgeport, on the south side of Chicago. A neighborhood of steelworkers and their families," she said, and for a moment it seemed as if she forgot that Angel was with her. "Funny the directions our lives have taken."

"Mrs. Martin, do you know anything about what Guy was talking about? Being cut out of the shopping mall, the hauling trucks when they were empty?"

"No, I don't," she said abruptly. "Zach's downstairs waiting for you. Guy was bandaged up and went off on his own somewhere."

"I'll being going, then."

"For another ten years?"

"Maybe."

"Good luck, then."

She kissed Angel on the cheek. As Angel walked out the door, Mrs. Martin suddenly stopped her.

"I never told you how sorry I am about the deaths of your parents," she said. "It must have been a terrible shock and a great loss."

"Thank you," Angel said. "It's been difficult. But it must have been difficult for you and for your husband. Losing two very special friends."

"It was very hard for me."

"But not for your husband? I thought my father and he were the very best of friends."

"Oh, dear, no, they hated each other in the worst kind of way."

"Why? I always heard these wonderful stories about how they went into business together. Your husband ran the trucking and materials end of things and my father always handled the construction and sales. I thought they were friends even before they went into business."

"They never told you about what happened before we were married," Jeanne said, lapsing for a second time into a distant memory that only she could see. "I was a beauty, then."

"You still are."

"Not like then. I could have any man I wanted, in or out of Bridgeport. But I had grown up poor, an orphan passed around from family member to family member, and I was determined to marry a man with a future.''

''And?''

Mrs. Martin suddenly became aware again of Angel's presence.

''And the doctors say that he's got a few more months, at any rate.''

''GOT YOUR PURSE? It's time to go.''

Zach ran his fingers through his thick hair and tugged at the banded collar of the sage silk shirt he had borrowed from Guy's closet upstairs. His own shirt he had simply thrown away, recognizing as soon as he had pulled off his suit jacket that blood had soaked completely through the familiar soft cotton.

He would have liked to have had time for a shower, a chance to run downtown to his own apartment for some much-needed sleep. But of course, there was no time.

The fight in the Sciopellis' foyer had brought home the urgency of the situation.

He had to persuade Angel to leave, and once that was accomplished, he needed to get to her on the next flight out of town. Of course, she would do what he wanted—after some persuasion. When she was young, she had always assumed he knew best—and now he counted on that instinctive, feminine reliance on his judgment.

She came down the steps, but lingered thoughtfully at the acorn balustrade just a little too long for his liking. He tugged her hand.

"Come on, we need to talk. And then I've got you a seat on a plane that leaves in an hour."

She tugged right back.

"Did you ever hear about your parents' courtship?"

"Not much."

"Did you know that O'Malley knew both our fathers when they were growing up?"

"No, but it doesn't surprise me. Chicago's a small town in some ways. O'Malley and our parents were all about the same age, growing up in a blue-collar neighborhood close to their parish."

"Your mother was very beautiful. And had her pick of men."

"She still is beautiful, and if she snapped her fingers this instant there's a large segment of the male population that would come running," he said, adding impatiently, "This is very interesting, Angel, but we don't have to chat here. Let's get in the car."

"I talked to O'Malley," she said, glancing back at the conservatory where his father's daybed and reserve oxygen tanks were housed. The television, which would be left on until morning static, was lulling Mr. Martin to sleep. "I told him I was leaving."

"Good. Because I was going to have that conversation with him if you didn't. And my conversation would have been more contentious."

"But he said no. He said I'm to tape the ten o'clock meeting and try to shoot pictures of as many documents as I can find tomorrow."

"Did you tell him forget it?" Zach said, grinding his teeth so hard his jaw hurt.

"He hung up before I could tell him."

"Damn that man."

"But, Zach, he said you would pick up the film and the tape."

"Of all the arrogant, low-down..." He slammed his fist into his other hand. "I'll have it out with him tonight."

"No. Don't. He's right. I should stay. I want to stay. I'll have to get the tape I put in this evening out and replace it with a fresh tape. Will you take it in to O'Malley?"

Zach uttered an oath under his breath.

"And why are you supposed to do all that? And why am I supposed to willingly help?"

"Because he's got an inch-thick file of information about who I am, where I am, what I do with my life. I can't go back—he knows exactly where I'll be. Zach, there's no place safe for me to go."

"Yes, there is," Zach said. "I'll give you a safe place. I'll make you a safe place."

He held her in his arms, soothing her trembling. She hadn't allowed her fear to show, but now she let go. And he was there for her, bringing her into his protective warmth.

"I won't let anyone hurt you," Zach soothed. "I haven't for ten years. I've protected you and I'll go on protecting you."

"How have you protected me?"

"By staying."

She broke away from his embrace and looked up at him suspiciously.

"Angel, O'Malley hasn't got any state secrets. Your father always knew where you were," Zach told her. "He could have tracked you down and taken you back anytime he wanted."

"He could? O'Malley made it sound like he was doing me a great favor..."

"That's O'Malley for you."

"So my father knew."

"Yes, he was just as able as O'Malley to cause you trouble. More so, perhaps. You hurt his pride and his heart by leaving."

"And he knew where I was?"

"Yes. He wanted to track you down and bring you home. But I persuaded him to leave you alone and, for some reason, my staying was good enough for your father to leave you alone."

"Did you know where I was?"

"No, I never asked and I didn't want to know."

"Why not?"

"Because the temptation to find you, to come to you, to be with you, would have been too great. I forced myself not to ask. But I'm sure your mother would have liked to have known about how you were," he said, remembering the woman's last words as she lay dying. "She loved you very much, with her last breath she told me how much."

He didn't explain that Mrs. Sciopelli had asked her to continue his role as protector, a role he had lived for all his life.

Angel thought soberly of her mother.

"What about my brothers?"

"I'm sure if they didn't know where you were before, they will now. They have access to whatever's in your father's study, including any files or notes he may have kept. But I'll cut them the same deal. I stay, you go. I stay, you're safe."

"What kind of power do you have that your staying is so important?"

"I'm still not quite sure, but it's worked so far."

"Why couldn't you have done just as well by coming with me?"

"Because I have other people who need my protection," he said, quieting her with a kiss.

The tender taste of vanilla and sweetness was his reward, and he hung on to her, savoring every moment.

Making love to her had satisfied his ten-year-long thirst, but had also lessened his drive to send her away.

She's got to go! a voice inside his head warned.

"You're going to leave now," he said.

"I think I should stay."

He ground his teeth.

She had changed a lot in ten years and, although he was a man who often used his charm successfully to convince people to do what he wanted them to do, he didn't have the slightest clue how to handle this new Angel. He didn't have the slightest clue how to work his charm when he most needed to.

"Angel, please, do as I say. Trust me."

"This isn't the sixteenth century, you know. And I can make my own decisions," Angel replied.

"You're crazy if you stay."

She crossed her arms over her chest and tilted her chin pugnaciously. And he knew that simply telling Angel what to do had stopped working ten years ago.

But he still had one trick up the sleeve of his brother's shirt and he pulled it out now.

He kissed her again and she stubbornly reacted

with all the passion of a statue. But he had molded her tastes with his pleasure and she couldn't hold out for long. Her lips parted, she took his tongue into her mouth and he thought he might kiss her forever.

But really only a moment and then he would tell her to go, to do as he said, while her defenses were down.

But he heard the soft padding coming down the stairs and looked up to see two little pink bunny slippers.

"Oh, Anna," he said, breaking away from Angel. "Aren't you up past your bedtime?"

A young woman, wearing a pink flannel gown and limp pink ribbons in her pigtails came to give him a hug. Her face was flatly planed, without the high cheekbones and strong jaw of her brother Zach. Her eyes, the color of blue cotton candy, were almond shaped and gently reminded the observer that her options were limited, her innocence to be maintained forever.

"Yeah, it's past my bedtime, but when I heard your voice, I knew you'd want to see the outfit I put on my new Barbie."

She held up a Barbie doll fashionably dressed in sequins and tulle.

"Do you play Barbies?" she asked Angel. "'Cause I have really good Barbie dolls. Zach buys them for me. He just bought me the Malibu Beach House, but this one my mother got me."

"That's wonderful. Anna, do you remember me?" Angel asked gently. "I'm Angel. Angel Sciopelli."

"Oh, Zach's girlfriend," Anna said, nodding. "You used to go with us when Zach would take me to the beach."

"That's right."

"I thought you were dead."

"No, I'm very much alive."

"That's nice."

"Anna, that's really a glamorous outfit you put on the Barbie, but you'd better get back into bed," Zach warned softly. He kissed her forehead. "Sleep tight."

"And don't let the bedbugs bite!" Anna finished with a triumphant giggle.

Angel patted her hand. "Sweet dreams, Anna."

Anna walked up to the top of the stairs.

The couple turned to go.

"Angel?"

"Yes, Anna?"

"You're not coming here to take my brother away from me, are you?"

"No, of course not," Angel said, choking on her words.

"Because I'd miss him very much."

A violent series of coughs erupted from the conservatory.

Anna startled.

"Inga! Inga! I need my pills!"

"Uh-oh, Daddy's up. I'd better go. Good night. Zach, don't forget you're taking me to the zoo tomorrow! I want to see the monkeys."

A tall, blond woman in a white nurse's uniform hurried down the stairs, bobbing a hello to Zach. She ran to the conservatory.

"I won't forget," Zach said. "Don't worry, Anna, I never forget."

She beamed at him and then, on hearing her father's orders to his nurse, she ran upstairs. Zach took Angel's elbow and steered her outside.

Chapter Eight

At 6:00 a.m., the phone rang on the business line in the upstairs study. At the polished tiger maple conference table, Tony sat studying the blueprints for the shopping center. Grimacing at the interruption of his private time, he put down his cup of amaretto-flavored coffee on its saucer and reached a well-manicured hand to the ivory-colored telephone.

"Yeah."

"Know who I am?"

He hesitated only a moment.

"You're a jerk," he said, enraged.

"No, Tony, I'm your new best friend."

"Why am I talking to you?"

"Because I know who killed your parents."

"Who?"

A bitter laugh.

"Tony, that was good. Very good. You had just that perfect touch of innocence. Maybe if you go to trial, you can tell the judge to have mercy on you because you're an orphan.''

Tony said nothing, cradling the phone between his shoulder and head while he carefully rolled down his shirtsleeves and put on his cuff links. Twin sterling silver power drills, a gift from the president of the carpenter's union in gratitude for the sweetheart deal the union got from the Sciopellis.

He thought about his parents, about the dinner party, about the way his mother had gotten out of the back of the car first. She usually got out of the car last, after her husband, because he was such an impatient man and always wanted to be ahead of everyone wherever he was.

''I would think you'd be celebrating now,'' Tony, Jr., said bitterly. ''Is this a phone call to gloat?''

''Neither of us are the kind of men who have the time or the heart for celebrations. And I never gloat. I boast, I cajole, I bluster. But never gloat.''

''Then tell me what you want from me.''

''All I want is Guy, Jr.,'' the other man said. ''Bring him to me. And don't go cowboy on me. I want him alive. I'm taking him down.''

''Finally. But if he's alive he'll talk.''

''Not if I'm the one asking the questions.''

''So that's the deal?''

''That's the deal.''

''What are you going to do to him?''

"Put him away. Far away. Forever."

"Joliet?" Tony asked, referring to the state's maximum security penitentiary.

"Someplace like that. He'll get what he deserves, the Martin family will get what it deserves and I might, just might, break open a beer and toast our cooperation. Don't worry, I won't force you to join me. Beer is too lower-class for your tastes."

Tony pursed his lips and thought this new development over.

"I don't want anyone interfering with my business," he said, making a quick notation on the blueprint in front of him. "I don't want what my father had."

The responsive laughter was without humor.

"Tony, don't you see? That's the whole point of this conversation."

The line went dead and Tony stared at the phone for a long time.

"YOUR BROTHER IS LATE," Angel whispered. She opened the front door and welcomed Zach with a worried, distracted kiss. "My brothers are up in the study throwing a fit. They're saying all kinds of terrible things. They're furious."

Zach stepped into the cool, marble-tiled foyer. Outside, it was already hot.

"My brother doesn't exercise a lot of judgment,"

he noted. "He's probably sleeping off a terrible hangover."

"Well, O'Malley's going to love all of this," she said. "And he's going to get every word."

"How do you know?"

"Because I brought up a tray of doughnuts and coffee to them."

"I didn't know you were that domestic."

"I didn't know I was that brave," she said over her shoulder.

He grabbed her hand. "Or that foolish," he said. "You should have let me do it. What if they...?"

She ran a hand up his shirt, placing a single cassette the size of a matchbox into his pocket. She proudly patted it.

"They didn't. They couldn't. They were too intent on bad-mouthing your brother to pay any attention to me. The recorder is wedged between two books on the bookshelf—I looked like I was interested in literature. My brothers certainly aren't."

"If you insist on staying, I will be in charge of tapes."

"I'm more than decorative."

"Yeah, but your decorative is really good. And I'm the one in charge here. Now, ssshhhhh," he said, silencing her with a quick kiss.

They looked up to see Tony coming down the stairs. He wore a European-cut navy blue suit with a starched white shirt and yellow shantung silk tie. He smiled warmly at Zach.

"When I heard the doorbell, I thought it might be your brother," he said, pulling back his cuff to glance at his Rolex. "It's eleven o'clock. Whatever could be keeping him?"

"Maybe he's sleeping off a drink," Zach suggested. "He was in a lot of pain last night. Dr. Morgan gave him some pain pills. Add to that a few martinis and bing! my brother is incapacitated."

"Again. He indulges himself too often," Tony chided. "That's why we've been troubled by his working with us. His truckers are always late, his workers sloppy and he always seems to have trouble keeping current on his subcontractors."

"I'll tell him to shape up."

"This whole mess wouldn't happen if you were running your family's company. You're levelheaded, disciplined, but, ah! I forget myself. You don't have an interest in business."

"You're right. I don't," Zach said evenly, keeping his arm firmly, and protectively, around Angel.

"What would you do if you didn't have Guy, Jr., to run the Martin company?" Tony speculated.

"The Martin company would go out of business," Zach said.

Tony nodded. "So what are you two lovebirds planning for today?"

"We're going to the zoo with Anna."

"Hardly romantic, but very thoughtful," Tony said. "Tell your sister that Maria will bring over the scale model of the Winnetka Shopping Mall next week. We've gotten all the subcontractors and village officials onboard with the vision so we're not going to need it."

"Thank you," Zach said. "I don't know how you do it, but all your scale models for every project you've ever built have been just the right size for her dolls."

"I tell Salvatore to make them that way," Tony said, bowing slightly to acknowledge Zach's gratitude. "Now, Angel, will you be back home in time for dinner? Or shall I tell Maria that you'll be out?"

"I actually thought I wouldn't go to the zoo. Maria mentioned that she was going shopping. Maybe I could fix this evening's dinner."

"Oh, no, I won't have that," Tony said. "Mrs. Tobin will take care of that. I want you to have a good time while you're my guest. During the day, we'll just be talking business when Guy shows up."

"Maybe we could help," Angel offered. "Zach and I—if we sat in. Maybe defuse some of the tension?"

"I don't think so," Zach said, firmly squeezing her arm. "Anna was so looking forward to seeing you today."

"Besides, it's just a simple business problem," Tony said. "Our father has contracted with the Martin Trucking Company for years for all our hauling and trucking needs. We just disagree about how that relationship will continue."

"But your business meeting last night resulted in Zach's brother being shot," Angel reminded him, wincing at Zach. He let go of her arm. "A simple business meeting shouldn't end in violence."

"Oh, Angel, you must think we're savages or that we solve every problem with a gun."

"Why would you have them around?"

"Because we're in a rough trade. We work with a lot of transient men who can't get jobs elsewhere or with men who are by nature physical and think all problems can be solved with brawn and not brain. I myself carry a gun," he said, pulling back his suit jacket to reveal a small, thin shoulder holster that didn't interfere with the line of his clothes. "And so do Salvatore and Rocco. Guy has more reason than any of us—trucking can be a rough-and-tumble trade."

"But last night…"

"Last night was unusual. We were all a little overexcited. I can assure you that won't happen today. Zach, you've never shown an interest in our meetings before," Tony observed, eyeing him speculatively. "Is there something you're not telling me?"

"I'm not the one who's interested. Angel is. And I think she was just a little off put by last night's brawl. As for me, I just want my brother's safety guaranteed."

"You are so protective of him." Tony sighed. "Even when we were young, it was always you coming to his rescue but never the other way around. And the funny thing is that you don't have anything in common. It's as if you weren't even related."

"We are brothers and I love him. And I want to enjoy myself today," Zach insisted. "I can only do that if I know Guy isn't in any danger."

"You have my word," Tony said. "It's business and I'll control my brothers. And I'm sure with his firing arm out of commission, he won't be in the mood for fighting, either."

"Then I'll be going," Zach said. "Come on, Angel, we promised Anna."

She stared at him for several seconds, deciding whether to do as he asked or hold her ground.

"If you don't want to go, you could go shopping with Maria. I believe she's taking Isabel with her," Tony said. "They were saying something about Chanel having a once in a lifetime sale."

"I can't afford Chanel. Even on sale."

"Then here, let me give you some spending money," Tony suggested, pulling out a thick wad of hundreds. He pulled off a couple of dozen. "They have panties this year that cost a hundred dollars. I should know, I got the store charge from Maria's purchases. She bought seven—one for every day of the week.''

''Anna's going to be disappointed,'' Zach warned.

Angel looked at the bills Tony offered her—more than two months of her own salary—and for some reason, the thought of spending it on an item of clothing revolted her.

''No, Tony, thank you,'' she said, careful not to offend. ''But I think I really would rather go with Zach and Anna.''

''Have it your way,'' Tony said smoothly. ''But the offer's open, whenever you need spending money just tell me.''

''Thank you.''

Angel ran upstairs and got her purse. As she followed Zach to the car, she looked back once to the house. Tony stood in the doorway, observing them with his hands deep in his pants pockets. He nodded a farewell.

''I wish we could have stayed.''

''There wasn't any way to do that without Tony getting more suspicious than he already is,'' Zach said. ''And besides, I can't protect Guy from himself.''

Without putting you in danger, he added silently.

Chapter Nine

They drove four miles through Winnetka and Glencoe streets flanked by buckthorn and maple. Grand houses were set back from the street, often surrounded by a border of gaily colored perennials and wrought-iron fencing. Even with all the wealth in homes, the downtown of Winnetka was shrouded in gloom. Shops boarded up, For Lease signs in nearly every window, nobody there to see the charm of the Tudor-style buildings and brick-bordered sidewalks.

At the gate to the Martin driveway, Anna stood waiting. Zach slowed the car to a halt and slid down his window.

"Daddy was yelling again," Anna explained. "So I came out here to wait for you."

Zach got out and let her in the back seat.

"Sometimes I think he doesn't like me."

"That's not true," Zach said.

"Well, he can't make me unhappy because today

we're going to the zoo," Anna said. "Can we see the monkeys first?"

"Sure," Angel said. "Are they your favorite animal?"

"Yeah."

"Mine, too."

The two women talked about animals while Zach walked up to the house to tell his mother he was taking Anna. When he returned to the car he had a disturbed expression.

"Can we listen to the radio?" Anna asked.

"Okay," Zach agreed, and he turned on a rock-and-roll station. He leaned close to Angel and whispered in her ear. "My mother says that Guy didn't return home last night. It's not unusual for him—he likes to party—but it's not good."

"Should you go looking for him?"

"I called his office, but they haven't seen him. I don't have a clue where else he'd be."

"What can we do?"

"Nothing," Zach said. "At least, not for now."

Angel tilted her chin up. "Then let's not think about it. We should make this a nice day for Anna."

They didn't speak of family matters for the rest of the day. Instead, they devoted themselves to Anna and, in doing so, rediscovered a lighter side to themselves, the side that had been left behind in childhood.

They walked through the zoo, rented a lagoon paddleboat for an hour and ate animal-shaped French fries with their lunches at the boathouse.

After stuffing themselves, they drove down to the Sears Tower, and while Anna and Angel took the elevator up to the top-floor observatory, Zach walked down the street to drop off the tape with O'Malley's secretary.

"Where is he?" Zach asked.

"Some kind of meeting with the mayor," said the dyed redhead at the desk in front of O'Malley's office. "Betcha want to know what it's about."

"Of course I do."

"Only for you, Zach, and only because you're cute. Although that's not going to do me any good because I'm too old for you."

"Seventy isn't too old," he said easily. "Seventy is when a woman is just hitting her prime."

"Keep talking, charmer. You're the only man who gives me a little flirt now and then," she said, and then leaned forward in her desk until her mouth was near his ear. "The mayor wants action on the Sciopelli murders. Now."

"Why's he so hot on it?"

"Because they think that if it looks like the Sciopelli company is weakened in any way, other guys are going to come in."

"Gangs?"

She leaned backward and scared off a paralegal who had been approaching the O'Malley sanctum.

"Enough with my perfume already, Zach," she said loudly. "Get a girl your own age."

Zach gave her a courtly kiss on her powdered check and figured that she had given him every piece of information she could. It was enough to make him realize that danger could come from all sides.

When they dropped off Anna at the Martin home, she had to be awakened from a satisfying nap in the back seat.

"This was fun, Angel," she said. "When will we do this again?"

"Soon," Angel promised. "Soon."

"Thanks, Zach," Anna said, and ran up the steps into the house.

"Have you seen or heard from Guy?" Zach asked his mother at the door.

"No," she said. "I'm very worried. His office called several times. There's been some trouble on the Winnetka site."

"What kind of trouble?" Zach asked.

"Another trucking company coming in and telling our men they're off the job."

"Mom, it might be for the best if Guy didn't work on Sciopelli projects all the time. This happens a lot, trouble on the jobs. If he could do work for other people, maybe he wouldn't have these fights with the Sciopelli brothers."

"You always say that, but I'm still afraid."

"All right, I'll try tonight to track him down."

Zach and Angel found the Sciopelli house empty. Maria and Isabel must have been clearing out the famous French designer's Chicago showroom and the brothers would probably be at the site. Mrs. Tobin had left a casserole in the oven and had set the dining room table so Angel didn't need to do a thing.

Zach helped Angel carry her zoo souvenirs up to the guest room. Angel, dumping a lavender-colored teddy bear on the bed, turned around.

She kicked off her sneakers. "Come here," she said, and she sauntered confidently to him. She tugged at his tie playfully, as if he were a puppy on a leash.

He reached back to shut the door.

She kissed him, the way he liked to be kissed. The way no other woman in ten years had learned to kiss him. She opened her mouth to him, offering him her soft, wet vanilla-scented flesh. He pulled away with a rich sigh.

"You want to make love on a bed?" he teased. "Isn't the chaise in the pool cabana exciting enough for you?"

She ran a delicate hand up his shirt. "All right,

it's a little kinky," she conceded. "A bed, sheets, pillows. It's so..."

"Wonderful," he said, sweeping her up in his arms and carrying her the scant three feet to the bed.

With one hand he yanked back the Battenburg lace comforter, while with the other he gently placed her on the white-on-white monogrammed sheets beneath.

"Wait, I've got sand on me from the playground," Angel warned. They had squeezed in a trip to the Lincoln Park playground and the North Avenue Beach.

"I love sand on a woman," Zach growled.

He had a moment of self-consciousness when he realized that he seldom smiled, even more rarely was playful, but that Angel had given him back that part of himself.

In the middle of turmoil, she had made him see that life could be enjoyed. He kissed her once on the forehead in gratitude, once on the cheek in reverence to her beauty and innocence and then pulled the sweetness from her lower lip as if she were the lushest of fruits.

Heaven! He sat astride her as he tugged off his suit jacket, which was specially tailored not as a fashion statement, but because it hid his shoulder holster effectively. Even in the appellate division of the district attorney's office, he was required to carry a gun. He never used it.

He unstrapped the holster, marveling at her beauty. At the way the light from the dying sun seem to sprinkle gold dust in her hair. The pink of her cheeks that was like the underside of a newly blooming rose. The way her mouth opened in anticipation of his next kiss. The roundness of her breasts and the slim curves of her stomach.

He struggled with the holster and leaned across her to put it on the nightstand.

He froze.

He felt the blood in his legs still, even as his heart sprinted and the roar of his pulse nearly drowned out her question.

"What is it, Zach?"

He stared at the flowers on the nightstand.

She followed his gaze.

"Oh, that's pretty," she said. "Mrs. Tobin must have put them there."

"I don't think so."

The crystal vase was filled with a voluptuous arrangement of roses, tulips, daffodils, daisies and marigolds.

They had one thing in common: every bloom was yellow.

He snapped his holster back into place and, with the sharp speed of a predator, he reached out, crushing a yellow rose bloom in his hand.

"What are you doing!?"

"We're getting out of here," Zach ordered, yanking her to her feet. "A yellow flower, any kind of yellow flower, means betrayal."

She tugged against him.

"All it means is that somebody put flowers in my room. Probably Mrs. Tobin."

"No, it doesn't mean that. It means you've been found out," Zach corrected. He grabbed his gun. "You're leaving. Now."

In the hallway, down the bridal staircase, Angel protested that he was being ridiculous. "You were just looking for any excuse to get me to leave," she said, outraged. "But I know what I have to do and I'm doing it. I'm staying. You can be the one to go. Stop ordering me around."

His response was a tightening of his fingers around her wrist, his logic was a gun drawn against the possible danger, his intentions were confined to getting her out of town.

"Angel, for once do what I tell you to do and don't put up a fight."

He grabbed her arm and pulled her with him, this time not sacrificing force for gentlemanliness.

"Zach, you're hurting my arm."

"Let's go," he growled, not letting up.

Knowing her reasoning wasn't getting very far against his brute strength, she stopped protesting and

did as he ordered. He hustled her along the stairs,
urging her faster. The door was scant inches away.

And then he heard the slight clearing of a throat.

Tony walked into the foyer.

He stood with his arms crossed over his chest,
blocking the front door.

Chapter Ten

"Where the hell do you thinking you're going?" he asked, his gentle tone belying a subtle hostility.

Zach pulled Angel behind him.

"We're leaving," he said evenly.

"I think not."

It was then that Angel believed Zach, understood the tiny bruised petals that clung to his pant leg.

She looked for a way out, but Rocco and Salvatore stood on the staircase, reaching into their jackets for their guns.

Salvatore wouldn't meet her eyes and she nearly felt the familiar surge of protectiveness. And then she remembered he had a gun pointed at her.

"She's leaving," Zach repeated.

"She can after we have a little talk," Tony said. "But we'll call her a cab when the time comes. You won't be available to drive."

Zach stiffened. "All right, what do you want, Tony? Lay it out. All of it."

"Justice," Tony said, his voice tremulous. "Someone in your family killed our parents and there's really only one punishment we think is sufficient. And I'm not waiting for the courts to get around to it. Criminals get all kinds of appeals. Delaying justice. You would know all about that, wouldn't you?"

"I'm not the enemy, Tony."

"I differ with you on that. Put your gun down on the floor. Nice and easy."

"Tony, wait!" Angel cried.

"I didn't do it," Zach said firmly, placing the gun down on the cool tile. "I didn't have anything to do with your parents' killing. And no one else in my family did, either."

"Then you won't mind going up to the study to hear a tape we have been sent."

Tony walked past the couple, confident that they wouldn't bolt. He paused once, pulling a slim tape recorder from the inside pocket of his suit.

"I think you forgot something," he said, handing a thin cassette to Angel. He yanked the thin tape all the way out so that it looked like a plate of spaghetti on his hand.

She took the cassette.

"Damn you," Tony said, without any emotion.

Zach jerked reflexively, ready to defend her name. But Angel held him back, reminding him with the pressure of her fingers on his chest that he had more to defend her from than bad words.

They followed Tony to the sumptuously furnished study, with its lingering scent of amaretto and cigars. Salvatore and Rocco took guard positions behind the armchairs that Angel and Zach were directed to. Tony sat on the chair behind his late father's desk. He leaned back comfortably and put his tasseled loafers up.

The desk was clear of all paperwork and knick-knacks. Instead, a slim recorder was placed on the leather desk pad. He flipped it on.

"This is a man worth listening to," he said.

"Tony, why do we have to do this?" Rocco asked.

"We have to do this," Tony said.

In a dull monotone, as if reading from a prepared text, a man identifying himself as Marcus Jones claimed that a go-between to the Martin family had offered him fifty thousand dollars for the shooting death of the elder Sciopelli.

"The man paid me twenty-five thousand in wrapped tens and twenties on our handshake," Marcus said. "And twenty-five thousand dollars was made available to me when the job was done."

Tony flipped off the recorder.

"So let's talk to this guy," Zach challenged. "Face-to-face."

"Can't. He's already gotten his…" Tony held a finger to his forehead and mimicked a trigger pull. "His justice. When I got the information about the killer, I didn't wait for the criminal justice system. There's too many lawyers like you to protect him."

Angel shivered at the horror of it.

"Who shot him?"

"Marcus?" Tony asked. He glanced up at Rocco. "That's not a nice question, Angel."

"A better question is why," Zach said. "Why would any of us kill your parents?"

"Business, jealousy, issues of the heart, who knows the heart of a stone cold killer?" Tony mused, pulling open the middle desk drawer. "Now enough talk. Angel, here's a plane ticket to Des Moines. And cab money to get you to Davenport. That is where you live, isn't it?"

Angel gasped.

"How did you…?"

"I will always know where you live," Tony said firmly. "And I have father's files. Congratulations on graduating from college by the way. Being class valedictorian while working nights at the diner was a real accomplishment."

Angel ignored the compliment. "I'm not leaving

Zach And I don't believe he did it or even knew that it was going to be done. He's too honorable a man.''

"He left you stranded in Vegas ten years ago. I wouldn't call that honorable.''

"I've forgiven him.''

"Can you forgive him killing our parents?''

"I don't have to because he didn't do it.''

"You think Anna managed this one?''

"No, of course not.''

"Mrs. Martin, or perhaps Mr. Martin weaned himself off of oxygen and painkillers long enough to think this one through?''

"No, of course not.''

"And Guy?''

Angel glanced at Zach. She felt like a traitor thinking that his brother could have done it. But he could have, couldn't he?

"He could have done it," Angel said. "So why don't you leave Zach out of this?''

"No, Angel, don't," Zach said. "This is not the way to get me out of trouble.''

"Ah, always ready to come to his brother's defense," Tony said. "Admirable, really. So which Martin brother did it or did they both?''

"I don't believe any of this," Angel said. "I don't believe either of them did this.''

"Let's agree to disagree," Tony said, leaning forward to hand Angel her plane ticket. "Can you love a man who ordered your parents killed or whose brother, father, mother or even sister ordered your parents to be shot like dogs in the street?''

She opened her mouth, ready to defend Zach. But then her mouth closed. She didn't know what to say.

"Goodbye, Angel."

"I'm not going," she rallied.

"Really?" Tony looked at Zach.

And it took just an instant of eye contact for the message to be communicated to Zach.

"Go, Angel," Zach said. "Just go. I'm telling you to go."

"I'll make a decision when I—"

"Stop it!" Zach cried out, the blue veins on his forehead throbbing. "Angel, you'll do as I say. Get out of town. Leave this one to me."

"Having trouble keeping your woman in line?" Tony asked blandly.

Angel threw him her haughtiest look. "What's going to happen to Zach?"

"I don't know," Tony said. "I haven't decided. Zach, kiss my sister goodbye and if she won't do what you tell her to do simply because you tell her to do it, tell her there's one reason she's going to get on the plane and never look back, never talk to anyone, never show her pretty face in this town again."

"What is that?" Zach asked.

Tony rose to his feet and buttoned his suit jacket.

"Anna," he said.

"Anna?" Rocco said. "I thought your sister was not playing with a full deck."

"I thought she was going away," Salvatore said. "To an institution."

"No," Tony corrected. "She's very much at home, at least as long as the Martin family has the resources. But she is very much in need of a guardian angel. And Zach has always been the very definition of those words."

"Tony, I want to talk to you," Zach said from beneath heavily hooded eyes. "Alone. Man to man."

Tony stared long and hard at Zach.

"You have woman problems," he said. "I know a little about that."

Rocco bristled and Salvatore looked away, embarrassed.

"But Maria and I got past it," Tony explained. "We had to come to an understanding about who was the boss. Sounds like you need to do the same thing."

"We're having that same problem here," Zach conceded, smiling in the face of Angel's outrage. "But I think I can solve this with a little help from you, Tony."

"All right, get her out of here," Tony directed Rocco and Salvatore. "Put her in the guest room and make sure she doesn't try something foolish."

"Zach, this isn't some little domestic dispute," Angel cried.

He shrugged negligently. "Just go, Angel, and stop whining."

Rocco picked Angel up by her elbows and hustled her out of the room. All down the hall, Angel tried to persuade her two brothers to let her go, to let Zach go—but her words were met with sullen grunts.

"So what did you want to talk about?" Tony asked, closing the door.

"I didn't kill your parents."

Tony reached back and picked up a decanter from a tray on the bookshelf behind his desk. He poured a sherry glass full for himself, then offered one to Zach and raised an eyebrow when his guest declined. He took his glass to his desk.

"I'm not stupid enough to believe you did," Tony said. "You've always had more than your share of scruples. But that leaves your brother and I'm not at all surprised that he'd do it."

"He didn't."

Tony drained his glass. "You're suggesting your dad, who can barely heave his body from one end of the room to another? Or maybe your mother, the former Miss Bridgeport of 1960, who probably takes ninety minutes to get herself made up for breakfast? Or perhaps your sister who is the mental age of an eight-year-old?"

"None of the above."

"I go with your brother."

"I don't think it's any of our family and I'm beginning to wonder if maybe you didn't have a hand in it. You had the most to gain, didn't you, Tony?"

"Did I really?" Tony asked, as if it were a philosophic matter. He stared at his glass, seemingly considering another. "I lost my father, my mother, my business mentor, my dearest defender, the most beautiful woman I've ever known—Maria will forgive me for saying that. I lost a lot."

"But look what you got in return."

"A lot of responsibilities. A business that's a pain in the…"

"I've heard it's got some profit to it."

"I would have those profits even were my father to have lived. I don't think I gained anything at all. I stand by my conviction that your brother double-crossed us. Murdered our parents in cold blood and now is too scared to face the consequences. Or perhaps he's planning a new round. This is war, Zach. War. He promised it to us, you heard him."

"Guy's not like that. He drinks and then he talks big."

"Here we part ways, Zach. He's just stupid enough and sure of himself that he'd think he'd get away with it. Question is—do I give in to my desire for revenge," he queried, pausing to consider the cigars in his desktop humidor, "or do I wait for the criminal justice system to take care of him?"

"Don't do anything to him."

"Zach, you're my closest friend outside of the family but you're asking a lot from me," Tony said. "You want me to ensure the safety of your sister, to forgive my own sister of being a spy in my house after I offered her my hospitality, and take a pass on your brother who has made me an orphan."

"It's a lot to ask," Zach conceded, leaning forward to snag a cigar from the humidor. He accepted a light from Tony. "But I want even more."

Tony puffed at his cigar and looked up, a glint of curiosity lighting up his otherwise coal dark eyes.

"How much more?"

"A favor."

"How much?"

"It's not like that. I want you to play a little game of make-believe. Kid stuff."

Tony chuckled.

"Kid stuff? I could use a little kid stuff in my life."

Chapter Eleven

Angel sat on the bed next to her duffel. She had tested every means of escape. The windows wouldn't budge, and Rocco scowled at her from the hallway when she inched open the door.

She raised her chin high as she heard noises approach in the hallway. Salvatore threw open the door and her heart soared as she saw Zach.

She nearly flew into his safe, strong arms. But Tony and Salvatore crowded into the door behind him. She satisfied herself with standing at Zach's side, breathing in his confident scent. Surely he could get them out of this mess, because she didn't have any ideas how to do it.

"Zach, what's going on?"

"We've agreed that we both find the murder of your parents repugnant," Zach said.

Angel opened her mouth and then closed it and then opened it again. She knew she probably looked like a surprised fish, and she was surprised, even if she wasn't a fish.

"Okay," Angel said cautiously. "The murder of our parents is repugnant. I can agree to that."

She looked at him for a clue as to how she was supposed to react. This had to be part of some plan he had. Zach never ran out of ideas, and she just had to figure out what he had in mind and play along.

But his impassive face gave her no clues and his gray eyes dared her to ask aloud the many questions she held inside.

"I think it's very bad that our parents were killed," she said, knowing her words sounded idiotic, though true. But she didn't know where Zach was headed with this. They weren't working as a team.

"We're going to leave open the question of who is responsible," Tony said, giving no indication of noticing his sister's persistent questioning glances at Zach. "But we can't jeopardize the completion of our Winnetka Shopping Mall while we determine the killer's identity. And we have other business interests to take care of."

"Legitimate ones?"

"Oh, Angel, don't be judgmental," Zach said.

Angel winced, but assumed he was playing some role that would eventually result in their escape.

"Sorry, Zach," she said, hoping that was the right response.

"Tony and I have come to an agreement," Zach continued brusquely, ignoring her apology. "An agreement about your future...and ours. I asked him for a tremendous favor and he agreed."

Ah, here it was, Angel thought—the escape hatch.

"It was easy to grant this favor because I trust Zach," Tony said. "He's an honest man, does what he says he's going to do, and I didn't need anything more than a handshake from him."

Angel stared openmouthed as Zach explained the terms of the new business partnership. Sciopelli would continue to do construction and sales of new projects, Martin would do materials and trucking.

Tony draped his arm around Zach's shoulder.

The two men talked easily, finishing each other's sentences. They had a camaraderie that extended to Salvatore and Rocco, who greeted the news of a partnership with backslapping and high fives.

Was that a smile on Zach's lips? This didn't sound like any kind of plan to her.

"I don't understand," she said flatly. "I thought you told me two minutes ago that he could be a murderer."

"He has finally broken his bad habit of defending Guy, Jr., when he shouldn't be defended," Tony said. "Zach knows Guy did it. And we'll turn him over to O'Malley. Satisfied?"

"I guess."

"Good. Now you've abused my hospitality long enough," Tony said, flashing his brilliant white teeth in a smile that would scare the devil. "Get out of here and don't come back."

"Tony, she's in shock," Rocco said. "She's not getting it."

"Even I don't understand it," Salvatore said quietly. "Zach's now our partner?"

"All right, I'll spell it out to you. The Martin family and Sciopelli family will finally work as partners," Tony said amiably. "Zach and us will have an empire. A business empire. It's a terrible, terrible tragedy that his older brother killed our parents and we are going to turn him over to the proper authorities. But we believe that out of tragedy can come good things."

Angel stared at Zach openmouthed. Only after a moment did she have the presence of mind to say, "But you can't possibly say you're going to do this."

"Angel, I've finally made my choices in life."

"You're just saying this because Tony made you or because you think it's going to get us out of trouble."

"Angel, if there's one thing you oughta know about Zach—" Tony chuckled "—it's that Zach is his own man. He doesn't get pushed around and nobody makes him do anything. Even me. And he never, ever makes deals that he doesn't intend on following through with. His handshake is golden. Right, Zach?''

"Right, Tony," Zach said, staring directly at Angel.

"Zach, what is going on?" she demanded.

"Tony, let me talk to her on my own," Zach said, pushing his new partner from the room. "It's all right, buddy, I'll talk sense into her. Woman trouble. You know what I'm talking about."

"Better get her in line," Tony warned.

Zach closed the door on her brothers.

Surely now, Zach would reveal himself, would take her into his arms and...

But he leaned negligently against the door, studying her from behind half-closed eyes.

"So, Angel, I made a deal. And now I want you to get out of here...assuming you want to go," he said. "A ticket to Vegas. Not Des Moines or Davenport. Don't go back there. Head for Vegas, spend a few nights clearing your head, play the tables a little and then start over. Someplace far away. Whole new life. A second chance, which is a helluva lot better than what you were faced with ten minutes ago."

"Did you sell your soul to Tony to save my life?"

"I didn't do anything that I haven't thought about for some time. Now's a good time for me to go into business with Tony. My father is going to die soon. My brother ordered the hit on your parents. And even if he didn't, Guy is too irresponsible to run our business. We need the money. Just think of the expenses taking care of Anna.''

"So you're going to run a trucking company?''

"My trucking company," he corrected. "My family's company. I have to do it. Did you know that Tony nearly hired a new trucking company because Guy wasn't bringing materials in on time?''

"What about their other business?''

"What other business?''

"Prostitution, drug-running, money laundering.''

"You've never had a head for commerce, Angel. Lots of things get done among businessmen that isn't looked upon kindly by the government. But why should a bunch of bureaucrats in Washington be sticking their noses in our business?''

"You sound just like my father.''

"No, Angel, I sound just like my father. But my father and your father were very much alike. And I am cut from the same cloth.''

"I don't believe you," she accused. "You're no friend of Tony, and you've never truly respected your father. Just last night you were telling me about how you had to warn him to not touch your mother or Anna.''

"Sure, I don't believe in a man striking a woman,

but that doesn't mean I'm not willing to fulfill my destiny, to take care of my family. O'Malley's never going to trust me, I'm never going to have a future in the D.A.'s office. So why shouldn't I?''

"You can't do this. You're not that kind of man."

"You've been gone for ten years," he explained. "You have no idea what kind of man I've become. Just as I had no idea what kind of woman you had become. I like my women a little more deferential, a little more concerned with their man's needs, a little more domestic. You don't take orders too well, Angel. You have a problem with authority figures."

"You like your women to be children."

He shrugged, conceding that she was right. "You've changed, Angel. And it's not all for the better."

"But we made love. Didn't you feel anything?"

"Sure. But I've had a little bit more experience than you. Enough to know that when the earth moves it doesn't necessarily mean wedding bells and true bliss."

"You've chosen."

"Yes, I have."

For the first time, Angel started to believe him.

"Angel, there are a lot of men and women who have worked for the Martin company their whole lives. People depend on the Martin company. How can I leave them with no one to run it?"

"So you're doing it for them?"

"Yes. And for Anna, who needs a lot of care. And for myself. I need to do something with myself. I've been standing on the tightrope for too long. It's time to stop the balancing act."

"And what about us?"

Zach shoved his hands in his pants pockets.

"You can stay." He shrugged, as if the matter was of little concern. "I'm not sure I'm ready to settle down, but maybe in a few years we could get married. We'd live in my father's home. You'd have to stop being so independent. I won't have a wife who works outside of the home. I want a lot of children, too. I'd raise them to join in the business when they grew up."

That prospect was the most chilling of all and deflated Angel's resistance to his new plans.

"You'd be a criminal," she said, shaking her head sadly. "Because that's what Tony is, in the end. That's how he does business. He's a thug. And you'd become one, too."

"Don't put it so coarsely."

Angel felt as if she'd been slapped. Where was her Zach? Where was the man who knew right from wrong? Where was his honor? Had she been wrong about him?

"And if I don't stay?"

"Start running. And don't stop," Zach said.

"Don't go back to Iowa. Too many people know where you've been. Don't let them know where you're going."

"You can't mean any of this," Angel exploded, coming to him. She shoved him against the wall, giving in to the animalistic instinct that she could knock sense into him. But when her hands touched his flesh, he didn't budge. "You can't mean that you're going into business with Tony. If nothing else, there was us. You and me."

"What about you and me?"

She looked up at him in horror at his words, delivered with deadly calm.

"What do you think everything between us meant?" she asked.

"Oh, baby, it was good memories, a few laughs and some fantastic lovemaking," Zach said, caressing her hair.

"You're lying!" she cried. "Zach, you're either lying or you've turned into a monster."

His face reddened as if she had slapped him.

"This is reality, Angel. Face up to it. I watched you go to Vegas. Ten years ago. And, baby, I'm telling you to leave me now. Just like then. But this time you'll know I'm not coming with you."

"Kiss me first."

He started, showing—for the first time since he had entered the room—a primitive fear.

"Why?"

"Kiss me first, before I go," she challenged, sensing her advantage. "Your kisses won't lie to me."

He did, his lips hard and bruising, his arms fiercely squeezing hers. Her arms hurting as much as her feelings, she struggled against him, but he had her right where he wanted her.

In his own sweet time, he relinquished her as if she were of no more interest to him than a day-old newspaper.

"So, am I a liar?" he challenged lazily.

"Monster," she corrected, rubbing her aching arms.

"Maybe so," he said. "Get on a plane. Get out and stay out. Don't come back to Chicago for anything, Angel, because you've run out of second chances."

And without another glance, he slammed the door behind him. She looked back at the table, at the yellow flowers. The tulips were drooping, the roses brown around the edges. She would hate yellow flowers for the rest of her life.

A gentle tapping on the door and Rocco announced that her cab was here.

"Rocco, please, you can't believe that anyone in the Martin family would want Mother and Father dead," she said when she came out into the hallway. He wouldn't meet her eyes. Instead, he picked up her suitcase, mumbled something unintelligible and headed downstairs.

"Salvatore, you can't believe this," Angel said to her loitering brother.

"I heard the tape the same as you," he said, shrugging. "I don't know what to believe anymore. Just get out, Angel. And remember, you're the lucky one to have a chance to go."

She hugged him, even though he tried to duck her. He had always thought he was too old for hugs. But when her arms were fast about him, he responded.

"Angel, I won't see you again," he said. "But have a good life. A quiet life. A boring life. I think it wouldn't be so bad to have boring."

He broke away from her and, without a backward glance, walked to the study.

Chapter Twelve

Two hours later, at the door of the Bella Winnetka restaurant, Tony held Maria's sable fur wrap for her. The wrap had been sent up that afternoon by a swank Michigan Avenue furrier.

He was so proud, so happy and so relieved. He had come out on top. Where he belonged.

"Tony, I don't need this fur tonight," Maria said. "Don't you think sable looks a little…gauche in summer? Especially after your parents' funeral? And after I spent all that money at Chanel today?"

"Nah, it looks great. Have to keep you warm," he said, knowing he was spoiling her and knowing that he wanted to spend the rest of his life spoiling her because it kept her happy. Her happiness was the one calm thing in his life. "Besides, a sable lets them know that we're successful."

"But I feel so terrible you getting this present for me only two days after we've buried your parents."

"Better to feel terrible in sable," he quipped, not telling her that he was actually in a celebratory mood this evening.

He nodded at his assistant, who glanced out the door to the men at the waiting Jaguar convertible.

"All clear, Tony," the assistant said.

The street was cooler than the restaurant, heavy with Lake Michigan mist. Winnetka was a small suburb and had only a few streetlights. Tony made a mental note to tell the village's streets department that they'd need more once the shopping mall was opened. He pictured something quaint, like the gaslights of olden days.

Maria could find them—she was good at tracking down beautiful things. He was really starting to appreciate her good qualities, especially since they had put their marriage back on track.

He escorted Maria to the door of the black Jaguar. He signaled his men that they could get into their cars—the twin Caddies parked across the street.

Tony turned around, feeling Maria clutch his sleeve.

"Tony, you go on in the car, I just want to look at that window," Maria said, pointing to a boutique. A glance at her charges this past month had informed Tony that this was her favorite shop. Maybe he could persuade the manager to open a new shop in his mall with a little kickback on Maria's purchases.

Funny how his mind always turned to business. His father would be proud of him.

He shuddered as he thought of his father lying dead on the parkway in front of the restaurant where they had planned their celebration.

"Sure, you go look. I'll get the car nice and cool for you," he said, marveling at her capacity to spend money and think about spending money.

He got in the car, and nodded to his men, then remembered that they couldn't see him through the tinted glass. He turned the ignition.

Something felt funny at his fingertips, like the wiggle of a fish about to escape his grasp.

And then Tony looked one last time at his beautiful wife, his only regret that he couldn't see her face once again, as she turned away to look at the display of sweaters.

"I love you," he said, knowing that she couldn't hear him.

There was an explosion, the shouts of Tony's men scrambling out of their Cadillacs.

One of Tony's bodyguards tackled Maria, just as she turned to see the bonfire, just as she tried to enter the flames to pull her husband to safety.

THE MARTIN TELEPHONE rang. Inga, the night nurse, picked it up in the conservatory and held the receiver to Mr. Martin's ear.

"Hello," he said.

There was a silence and then a fumbling at the other end.

"Hang up, Jeanne, it's for me."

The extension was put down.

"So?" Guy asked.

"You didn't tell me about Tony," a woman's voice said.

He glanced at Inga, straining to catch a glimpse of her full, round breasts as she leaned toward him with the phone. He might be too old to do anything, but he still liked to look.

"What about him?"

"He's dead."

Guy smiled, and Inga, misinterpreting again, looked down to see that the zipper of her nurse's uniform revealed too much. She sat up straight and said something in Swedish that he guessed was a rebuff.

"You got your money," Guy said. He didn't have to choose his words with too much care. Inga barely understood English. "And there will be more. You keep the five when the job's complete. We agreed to that."

"I don't like surprises."

"Life doesn't have any more surprises in store for me. And this job doesn't have any more surprises in store for you. Let's just be done with it."

The woman hung up first.

He didn't like that in a woman, but she was a professional and he'd have to live with it.

ZACH UNLOCKED THE DOOR of his Gold Coast apartment and flipped on the light.

He switched on a Tiffany torchère in the living room and snagged a cola from the refrigerator. Then he walked back into the bedroom and listened to the messages on his voice mail. Two from O'Malley, demanding he do his job without so much complaining, and saying the tape from the Sciopelli study from the previous evening was useful and when were there going to be more.

A third message was from a woman in his building saying she just happened to have two tickets to the opera and her mother, with whom she usually went, was unable to attend.

"Would you give me a call?" she purred. "I just need an escort for the evening. No pressure. This isn't a date, really. Just opera."

He shook his head. The woman had asked him out on three other occasions—and each time he had had to respectfully and diplomatically decline. Somehow it had been off-putting to have her doing the pursuing.

Maybe Angel was right—maybe he was a man better suited for the sixteenth century.

Four hang ups.

And then his brother.

"Zach, Zach, it's me. Pick up, won't you? Dammit, I need to talk to you. I need your help. I know I've been a jerk sometimes, but this is important. Pick up the phone. Now. Please."

Guy was already feeling the heat. No doubt the Sciopelli brothers were looking for him.

Zach wished he could do something for his older brother, but if Guy had ordered the hit on the Sciopelli family, Zach's ability to shield him was limited. Unless he could get him to O'Malley. Even then, in the arms of the law, a jail-house assassination wasn't unheard of.

But what if Guy was innocent?

He closed his eyes. Zach had already sold his soul to protect Angel's life. And sister, Anna. And his mother and the scant remaining days of his father.

And then there was his brother.

A pattern in their relationship had been that Guy would get in trouble. Big trouble. Little trouble. Woman trouble. Business trouble. Drinking trouble.

And Zach, though younger, would get him out of it. Whether it was beating up a schoolyard bully or gently telling a woman that she was wasting her time with Guy, Zach would work a miracle.

And Guy would express his gratitude and then go out and break every promise he had made to do better. They had left Dr. Morgan's Glencoe home with a bottle of painkillers, a bandaged shoulder and Guy's vow that he would be a perfect gentleman at the meeting with the Sciopelli brothers.

How long could he protect Guy from his own stupidity?

The devil never keeps his end of the bargain, O'Malley had said. And though he had bargained with Tony to let the law take its due from Guy, Zach knew the devil would break his promise.

He'd have to find Guy and bring him in himself.

He heard a noise in the living room and he slid his gun from his shoulder holster.

A lot of people were counting on him living a good, long life—he had to take care of himself, he mused bitterly.

He slipped down the hallway noiselessly. He paused at the kitchen door. He was positive now he heard someone in the living room.

He took a deep breath, flicked the safety on the gun, rolled out onto the living room floor and trained his sights on a shadow moving in front of the door.

Groaning, he caught the safety and threw his gun to the ground.

"I thought I told you to get out of here, Angel."

"You know I never do what I'm told."

"Well, you can't stay with me, because I like an old-fashioned girl. The kind who does what her man tells her to do." He had chosen his words carefully, hoping to antagonize her.

But when she turned, her blond hair fanning out behind her, she was as cool and self-possessed as the woman with the tickets to the opera.

"I'm not staying," she said.

"So what'd you do? Forget something?" He picked himself up and put his gun back in his holster.

"Yeah, I forgot this," she said, and came into his arms.

She kissed him. Hard. Physically. With none of the hesitations and inexperience that she had shown a million years ago, last night. One leg brushed up his thigh, one hand caressed his hard, but sensitive abdomen. He felt an immediate reaction in his groin.

She had learned how to kiss. And he had been the man to teach her.

"Oh, no," he protested, pulling away reluctantly but firmly. "You're getting on a plane out of here. Come to think of it, I'll drive you to the airport myself. Just to be sure. You have this funny habit of staying when you don't belong."

"My plane leaves in two hours," she said, wrapping her arms around his neck.

"So I'll buy you a hot dog at the concessionaire," he replied, taking her hands right back off his neck.

"No, we have two hours, Zach. That gives us just enough time."

"For what?"

"For this."

And she kissed him again. This time she didn't let go. "I'm not going back without a goodbye kiss," she said huskily.

"No, Angel, you need to make a life for yourself," he said, pulling her fingers out from behind his neck. He knew just how dangerous her kisses could be. "You need a husband and children and a home of your own. Don't look for any of that here, baby. I can't give it to you. Make your life somewhere else."

"But, Zach, that's the point! I haven't made my life in the ten years I've been gone. I've been waiting for you, I've put things on hold for you, I've always had in the back of my mind an idea that you are my husband."

"You've done a lot with your life," Zach protested. "You've finished college, you're a professional in a career, you're—"

"I haven't stopped loving you. And I can't even stop now, when I know I should." She stepped closer, spreading her thin, pale hands across his chest.

His skin pulsed beneath the soft fabric of his shirt. "You'll find someone else."

"I've dated a few men and I've thought things might become serious a couple of times. But I feel as if I'm cheating on you somehow. Besides, I always judge a man by you and then I'm disappointed when he can't measure up to the standard you've set.''

"Measure up to me?'' He chuckled. "Angel, tonight I sure don't feel like anybody's standard of what a man should be.'' Then he realized he was softening. Showing a true side of himself. That's not what she should see now. That wasn't how to play it. "So, other men don't measure up, do they?'' he asked, tilting his chin up in a show of pride.

"No, they don't,'' she said, dropping her head to one shoulder, revealing the quickened pulse of her neck. "Maybe that's what comes from being promised to a man on your christening day. And when we made love ten years ago, I really felt as if you were making me your wife. It meant that much to me.''

"But I abandoned you by sending you off to Vegas on your own. Abandonment is grounds for divorce in all fifty states.''

"I could stay.''

"You don't take orders very well. This is your goodbye, Angel. Anything else would be wrong.''

Just as he would lean down to kiss the blue line that throbbed beneath the pale skin of her neck, she pulled away from him and sauntered across the living room floor.

"Zach, just this once. Please, just this once.''

"Why do you want it so bad?''

"Because I need to say goodbye. I need there to be a goodbye.''

"It would be wrong for you," he said truthfully. It would also be wrong for him. He wasn't sure how he could retain his self-control.

"Do you want to say goodbye to me?"

"Sure, baby," he said. "Goodbye."

"No, Zach," she said, turning and wagging a finger at him. "Say goodbye to me. Really say goodbye to me."

"I thought that was a pretty good goodbye."

She lazily approached him. She kissed him, drawing in his sweetness, teasing his tongue with hers. She was bold, she was sensuous, she was in charge whether he liked it or not and she wasn't leaving him until she got what she wanted.

"Zach, just this once," she said when he pulled away. "And then I'll leave you. I promise. I'll walk right out that door, get on a plane and never see you again. Because I shouldn't see you again even if I wanted to. You're telling me you're a dangerous man, a man with no scruples. And I'm trying to believe you—but all I have in my head is the Zach who does his best to do what is right."

She pulled her T-shirt up over her head. Underneath was a plain white bra. She thrust her breasts forward, making no secret of the pleasure she gained at the way his eyes slid down from her face in open appraisal. He wanted her—even as his mouth sputtered a plea that she put her clothes back on.

She was the kind of woman who had kept herself

under wraps for so long that she had begun to doubt that she had the kind of feminine power that other women took for granted. But one look at Zach's distress confirmed her hold on him.

And confirmed for Zach how much he must resist.

Zach groaned. "Angel, if you take off your clothes, I'll…"

Disobediently, she unzipped her jeans and slid them down her hips. Her stomach was flat, and had the untried quality of a woman who had never borne children. She shimmied suggestively to kick the jeans away and he moaned aloud.

"Put your clothes back on."

"Zach, if you're as unscrupulous as you want me to think, you should have no problem bedding me now."

"We shouldn't."

"What—you have qualms all of a sudden?" Angel taunted. "You're in business with my brothers, you're turning your back on the district attorney's office, you've rejected the law and now you're hesitating about having sex with a woman who's just said she wants to?"

"It's making love."

"It depends on what kind of man you are."

Chapter Thirteen

For a brief instant, he saw her doubt—was he that kind of man? Sometimes he had wondered about himself. After all, he was a strong, virile, handsome man. Women were easy with Zach, and he could have his pick—glamorous women, exotic women, actresses, models, secretaries and lawyers. Still, he had turned his back on the nightlife because he, like Angel, had experienced a niggling feeling of guilt, as if he were cheating on her every time he was with another woman.

"I don't excite you?" she asked.

But the glitter in his steel eyes betrayed him, telling her he was definitely not bored by her display. The flick of his tongue across his lips assured her that while she might be only one of many women, she was the only one he wanted.

Funny, she exhibited no modesty in front of him.

"I can't, Angel, I can't."

"We did it the other night. Just what kind of man are you, Zach?"

She kicked her jeans out of the way and slid her fingers beneath the spaghetti strap of her bra. Dropping one over her shoulder and then another. Teasing him mercilessly. He slumped into the white denim slipcovered armchair and stared helplessly.

Enjoying her feminine power to entice, to excite, to entrance, Angel raised her hands and flipped her hair back from her face. A seemingly casual gesture, but instinctively she knew what she was doing. All she had to do was watch his eyes; the way his pupils dilated told her when she was doing something right.

That and the straining at his groin.

He was like an instruction manual opened to the page on how to torment a man.

She rubbed her hand across her shoulders, enticing his imagination with what his fingers could touch— if he only said the word.

Her breasts rose high, nipples taut and bloodred.

Zach growled and roused himself. In two strides, he crossed the living room and swept her up into his arms as easily as if she were a paper doll.

A stab of fear within her was immediately followed by an exhilaration she had never known. His face was close, his breath hot and sweet on her skin.

He would take her and she would finally be his.

"Dammit, Angel, you can't torment a man like this and not expect—"

"Oh, but I do expect." She pouted.

He took her lips, a kiss brutal with longing and nothing like the tenderness of their long-ago courtship.

This was a man's kiss and she responded as a woman—with an excitement that fired at her core like hot oil.

He carried her into the bedroom, kicking shut the door behind him. He dropped her on top of the bed, and if she was expecting a sudden tender declaration of love she got none.

He still thought he could do this his way.

He bore down on top of her, spreading her legs apart to accommodate his torso—his clothes rubbed rough against her delicate skin.

He caressed every inch of her as if desperate to mark her as his own, he suckled at her full breasts to bring the aching of her heart to fruition and he splayed his fingers possessively at the soft mound at her sex.

She should loathe him, she should reject him, she should despise him; she should get up, walk out of this apartment, out of this city, and never look back.

He wondered why she didn't.

"Now, Zach, now," she whispered, though she scarcely knew what she was asking for.

He didn't wait, his need for her so great. He tugged at his shirt and tie. Though she helped with trembling fingers, it was he who threw off his clothes as if he were a savage throwing off the last vestiges of an uncomfortable and despised civilization.

As he knelt above her, his thighs forcing apart her legs, Angel stared at his manhood, engorged with blood and pulsating with life.

"Now," she repeated, and she lay back on the comforter, her hand flat against her stomach to still her breathing. "Zach, I want you."

Assured of her readiness, he held himself above her, his sweat-slicked arms stiff like columns on either side of her shoulders.

His manhood paused at a point of resistance and then entered her in a breathtaking moment of mingled pain and momentous pleasure.

"Look at me," he commanded quietly.

She obeyed. His eyes glinted hard like silver, sparked at each thrust into her wanting body. She felt him stir a whirlpool of sensation.

As his movements quickened, bringing them closer to the moment of ecstasy, the color of his eyes softened like a watercolor. Mingling gray and dusty blue and dappled gold.

He called out her name.

She clawed at the powerful muscles of his back.

And then in a dazzling instant, they were electrified with pleasure. A pleasure that coiled like a spiral of stars. She looked into his eyes at that moment and he knew she saw into his soul.

She had found him out. It had just taken more than a single kiss for her to know him.

THEY LAY SATED but still wanting…everything.

As their breathing quieted, Zach reluctantly pulled out of her. "You still have to go," he murmured, laying beside her and putting his arms around her.

"What?"

"I meant what I said."

She shook her head. "I know you lied about being in business with my brother, I know you lied about the kind of man you are," she said. "You've been trying to persuade me that you're no good to make me walk out that door and never look back. But you can't lie to me when you kiss, when you make love to me. Now tell me what's really going on. Tell me the truth this time."

Zach stared up at the ceiling, watching the play of traffic lights.

"I have made a deal, Angel, but it's not the one I told you about."

He leaned against her spoonwise, feeling his breath touch her shoulder.

"What is the deal?"

"Why do you have to know?" he said, suddenly

tired of all the balancing acts he performed to keep so many people in safety. "Isn't it good enough for you to trust me and just go when I tell you to go?"

A dazzling pattern of red and blue light flew across the ceiling. At first Angel thought it was the aftershock of bliss. But Zach leapt to the window, separating the slats of the blinds to get a look. And then gave a murderous glance to the heavens.

"Police," he barked. "Get dressed."

She got up, looking back only once as he flipped the comforter over the bed.

She scampered to the living room, grabbed her clothes and slammed the bathroom door shut behind her just as the police hammered on the front door.

"Open up, Mr. Martin, we have a warrant for your arrest!"

"Coming, coming." Zach's muffled reply. "You don't have to knock the door down."

In the bathroom, Angel studied her face in the mirror. Her hair was tousled, her cheeks pink and the touch of mascara she had applied before dinner was smudged. She looked terrible, but in an odd way, she looked at peace.

She knew she would be his bride, forever, no matter what their fates. And that meant more than skillfully applied mascara or the most flattering shade of lipstick.

The barrage of sounds from beyond the bathroom

door made her guess there were three policemen, maybe more.

She quickly slipped on her clothes, running Zach's comb through her hair and wetting a washcloth to wipe under her eyes. When she came out of the bathroom, she found four uniformed cops prowling around the apartment. Zach was in handcuffs. His face hung low.

She ignored the open appraisal of the police, though she knew they were speculating about the intimacy between her and Zach.

Bucking against the cuffs, Zach jerked his head toward her suitcase. "Get going, Angel," he said. "You've got a plane to catch."

"What are you being arrested for?"

Zach shook his head.

The police officer eyed her and then cruelly spat out the answer. "Murder."

"He didn't murder my parents."

"Nobody said nothin' about your parents, lady."

"Whose murder?" Angel demanded.

"Ma'am, I was just sent down here to get him," the officer said. "We don't discuss charges with… hey, you're not his lawyer, are you? I didn't think lawyers had nighttime office hours," the cop said, pleased with his wit.

"She's not my lawyer," Zach responded for her.

"Zach, are they taking you to jail?"

"Just get out. For once stop being so damned stubborn and go!"

And he was taken away, the officers not bothering to close the door behind them.

She looked at her suitcase, at her little purse and at the empty living room. The smart thing to do would be to clear out now. Head west and keep going without a backward glance.

He had actually done her a favor telling her to get out.

She grabbed his car keys from the coffee table.

THE DEARBORN STREET precinct house was a squat gray block guarding the no-man's-land between the housing projects and the luxurious Gold Coast.

Angel parked Zach's car across the street, worried when a gang of street punks eyed the vehicle speculatively, and then pulled a twenty-dollar bill out of her envelope purse.

"There's more where that came from if the car's still here when I get back," she said.

A wide-eyed youth snatched the bill from her and shoved it into his jeans pocket.

"It'll be here," he promised.

She stopped at the processing counter to ask for help, but the desk sergeant was having a heated conversation over the phone about transferring some prisoners, and a beat cop came in with two men in cuffs.

The sergeant glanced up, saw the two competing interests and nodded an acknowledgment to the beat cop even while mouthing off an obscenity to the person on the other end of the phone.

Using the distraction, Angel slipped down the hall, looking in every doorway for someone who knew where Zach was.

At last, she found a woman cop with a pencil stuck behind her ear who jerked her head toward the stairs when Angel mentioned Zach's name. The second floor was nearly empty, with only the occasional uniformed officer passing her in the gray, fluorescent-lit halls.

"Zach, Zach, where are you?"

Angel nearly gave up and went back downstairs, and then she saw the woman on a gray metal bench at the end of the hallway. Her head was bowed, her face red and wet with tears, a fur coat around her shoulders dirty with ash and soot.

"Maria!" Angel cried.

Maria looked up, a glimmer of fear and—could it be?—anger in her face. And then she pushed herself up from her chair and came into Angel's arms with renewed sobbing and keening.

"What happened?" Angel demanded, soothing

her sister-in-law, stroking her hair. "Did you get hurt?"

Maria shook her head vehemently. "No, it's my Tony!" she exclaimed. "My beloved Tony! He went to start the car and..."

"Oh, no."

"Yes, it blew up. I watched my husband die! Now I am a widow!"

Angel closed her eyes to the bitter truth.

"How can so many bad things happen to our family?" Maria sobbed. "Why do we have to endure so much? I'm going to my family's home in Italy. I can't take this town anymore."

"Who did this?"

"You oughta know." Maria sniffed. "You loved that man."

"Zach? That can't be."

Maria's eyes narrowed with ferocious venom.

"The district attorney told me it was Zach. He ordered Tony's murder and I believe him. That Martin boy is a monster!"

"No! No! No! It can't be true. Please, it can't be. He worked for O'Malley."

"That doesn't mean he was a good man."

"He is a good man."

"No, Angel, he's a murderer and we let him into our home, offered him our hospitality. You were to be married to him. Your father was his godfather, his father was like an uncle to the whole family. Tony considered Zach his closest friend. I even liked him, although…'' She dabbed her eyes. ''Although I always had my suspicions about him.''

''He couldn't have done it.''

''Oh, but he did. And he's the one who killed Papa and Mama Sciopelli.''

''No, no, Maria, that can't be true! There must be some mistake.''

''Believe it,'' a voice said wearily. ''There's been no mistake. Except Zach's mistake—choosing the wrong side of the law.''

Angel looked up over her sobbing sister-in-law's head to see the grim face of Patrick O'Malley.

''And my mistake,'' O'Malley continued. ''In trusting you to be able to see the difference ten years had made in that man.''

Chapter Fourteen

"Your brother Tony was killed by a car explosion," O'Malley said, settling his weight into the gunmetal vinyl chair behind the desk in the police interrogation room. "It was instantaneous."

Angel squinted at the wide, framed mirror.

"Don't sweat that," O'Malley said. "There's no one there. This is nothing formal. This is just between the two of us."

"All right. So you can feel free to tell me everything."

"And you will tell me everything you know," O'Malley challenged, cracking an arthritic knuckle. "As a sign of faith in you, I'll go first. It happened outside the Bella restaurant. He was taking Maria out for dinner—they've had some marriage problems but your brother has been making a real effort to pull it together. According to Maria, they were doing something special because she had just completed some purchases of interior paneling for the mall project. Another celebration of the new shopping mall goes bad.''

"Were they by themselves?''

"Yes, just the two of them. Rocco was at home watching TV—Mrs. Tobin, the housekeeper, confirmed that. And Salvatore was at his drafting table, coming up with a new project.''

"I only left the house at seven o'clock by cab,'' Angel said, slumping into the gray folding chair on the other side of the desk. She felt weak and dizzy with shock. "Last I saw, Tony was fine.''

"And Zach was with him.''

"Zach was with him,'' Angel agreed cautiously. "And then Zach was with me.''

O'Malley raised his eyebrows. "Was he really? The whole time?''

"I found him in his apartment at nine. I was supposed to be going to the airport.''

"And then?''

"And then is none of your business.''

"We're supposed to be telling each other everything we know.''

"What you need to know is that Zach never left the apartment.''

"It probably makes no difference if Zach has an alibi—this was a professional job.''

"How do you know?''

"Tony had a brief dinner with Maria at the Bella Winnetka restaurant—they were inside for no more than an hour. His car was wired while he was inside. It was a liquid mercury ignition system—fairly advanced but commonly used by the pros."

"In the Jaguar?" Angel asked. O'Malley nodded. "But he had plenty of bodyguards. Any one of them would have seen someone tampering with the car."

"None of them are talking."

"Well, keep asking them."

"All we know is that as soon as Tony turned the key on the ignition—"

"But Tony never starts the car," Angel interrupted, thinking of how her father and brothers always asked a guard to start the car.

Her mother had, when Angel was young, explained this was because her father liked the car to be the right temperature when he got in—neither too hot nor too cold, but just right.

"Tony started the car because he was thinking more about Maria than about safety," O'Malley said. "According to Maria, he waved away the guards. She wanted to look in a shop window, and that momentary interest in sweaters is what saved her. She feels plenty guilty."

"But how could the bomb be wired when Tony had these guards around?"

"We don't know," O'Malley complained. "We'd

like the bodyguards to give us information about who had access to the car while Tony and Maria were eating, but none of them will talk.''

"Scared.''

"Yeah. Or guilty. At the very least they know who's in charge now.''

"Who's in charge?''

"It's not Rocco and Salvatore. They're not strong enough. Most people are looking to Zach.''

"Zach doesn't have the slightest interest in the family business.''

"He made a deal with Tony to share the business.''

"That's a lie.''

"Maria, Rocco and Salvatore think he did.''

"They may have thought he did.''

"But you know better?''

She thought of their lovemaking. "Yes.''

"You don't know anything, Angel. You're as innocent as they come. A real naif.''

"All right, so I'm naive enough to believe that Zach is innocent. Why don't you give me an education?'' she challenged. "Let's start with how you know it was Zach who killed my brother Tony.''

"And your parents. Let's not forget your parents in this.'' He wagged a finger at her. "We have some money traced to the Martin family—the bills had been spliced with a metal strip, kind of like a bar code, before they were included in a payoff to the Martins by undercover drug agents. The strips help us trace large movements of money to and from the Martin family. Fifty thousand in cash was taken out of a safety deposit box belonging to the Martin family in the week of your parents' deaths.''

Twenty-five on signing and twenty-five on completion, Angel thought, remembering the voice of Marcus Jones on the tape.

"Another half million was taken out of the box yesterday morning. That must have been Tony's death certificate.''

"Who went to the bank?''

"Anna.''

"That's not possible.''

"She was always accompanied by a woman—tall, well-dressed, wore a hat with a wide brim. She never signed for the box, kept her face turned away from the security camera and even wore dark shades. The bank clerk can't make a positive ID, but there's only one woman I know who takes Anna out.''

"Her mother.''

"And she did it for Zach.''

Angel shook her head. "I don't want to believe Mrs. Martin is guilty of anything, but couldn't she have just as well done it for Guy?''

"Angel, I'm banking on Zach because he's the smarter of the two of them. Guy, Jr., couldn't arrange a dinner party without some help. But do either of us really know?''

"I believe I do."

"And I believe I do. We need to be sure."

"I'm sure Zach is innocent."

"Sure because you had sex with him? Don't look so shocked. I'm not stupid. Or are you sure because you can't believe you would fall in love with a criminal? Angel, if women never fell in love with the wrong guy, the Poconos would go out of business, rice would only be used for cooking and we'd all be a helluva lot better off. Especially your brother."

Angel shuddered, thinking of her hysterical sister-in-law, who had been led away by Rocco, who had patted her hand and promised O'Malley that he'd get her a sedative.

"Where is Guy, anyway?" she asked.

"Hate to break it to you, Angel, but my best guess is that he's dead. I've had my men keeping their ears open—the last person to see him was Zach. Right after they left Dr. Morgan's house."

"Guy had a dispute with my brothers about business. He had a reason to kill them."

"If he killed any of your brothers, it would be like killing the goose that lays his golden eggs," O'Malley countered. "Don't you think it pains me to have to admit that someone in my office might be a traitor? Especially Zach. I had such high hopes for him—but maybe walking a tightrope between family and what's right is too much for a man.''

''He's a good man,'' Angel said softly.

''A man can change,'' O'Malley replied flatly. ''Zach started off with good motives. You love him, don't you?'' O'Malley asked. ''You love him even now.''

''I love him and I don't believe you.''

''If you knew that he killed your parents and your brother, would you still love him?''

''No, he wouldn't be the same man.''

''Then it's a matter of proving to you that he did it or didn't do it.''

Angel stared at her hands, the fingertips still tingling from the feel of Zach's skin. She knew she still loved him. But could she love him if he were a murderer? Of course not. The possibility terrified her.

Angel looked up at the district attorney. Tears welled up in his eyes.

''He was like a son to me,'' he said softly. ''I didn't want to believe the evidence myself. Prove me wrong, Angel. Please prove me wrong. I hired him. I backed him up when everyone said to me that he was a Martin kid and couldn't possibly be any good. I've wanted to believe in him, even when he's such a private man that I didn't even know until I saw you two in the cathedral together what a damn torch he's been carrying for you. Give me a reason to believe in him, because I've lost the power to believe. I need you to prove him innocent."

"How?"

O'Malley swiped the back of his hand against his wet cheeks.

"He's refusing to see the lawyer his father sent for him and he's refusing to speak to me. I'd like you to get him to talk."

She thought back to the way Zach presented his "deal" with Tony. "He won't talk if he doesn't want to."

"Make him talk. Figure out a way. You want to know, once and for all, who killed your parents, don't you? And whether the man you think you love is worthy of your love, don't you, Angel?"

She put her head in her hands.

"I swear to you if he's innocent, I'm giving you both your freedom."

"I've heard it before from you, O'Malley, and I don't believe it anymore."

"No, this time believe it. Real freedom. Witness protection kind of freedom. You can start over. And if you're wrong and he's a guilty man, you can put it behind you. Once and for all. It can be over."

"What do you have in mind?"

"MRS. MARTIN? It's Angel. I'm sorry to call so early in the morning. Were you up?"

"Oh, I've been up all night. Salvatore called me and told me about your brother. I'm very sorry, Angel. I'm sure Zach didn't have anything to do with it. He's a good man."

"I know, Mrs. Martin. I agree with you. But the law doesn't feel the same way."

"That's very troubling."

Angel looked down at the pay phone's ledge.

At the notes she had written to remind herself what to say—and what to ask.

"Mrs. Martin, the district attorney's office is going to ask for a half-million-dollar bail. They're really pushing for a conviction."

"Isn't the attorney handling that?"

"Zach refuses to talk to him. I think because it's the family lawyer. The one your husband uses," Angel said, choosing her next words with great care. "I think Zach might not trust him."

There was a long silence and Angel wondered if she and O'Malley had miscalculated.

"Maybe I had better come downtown," Mrs. Martin said, and Angel could barely conceal a smile.

She worked hard to keep her voice neutral.

"I think it would be a good idea if you did. He's scheduled for an arraignment at nine-thirty. I've gotten O'Malley to agree to a meeting a half hour before."

"I'll be there. Oh, dear, I just thought of something. I'm going to have to find someone to take Anna. I don't like to leave her here at home.''

"If you bring Anna downtown, I could stay with her while you try to talk sense to Zach. He should cooperate with O'Malley.'' Angel held her breath, waiting for Mrs. Martin's reaction.

"I agree with you, Angel, but you do the talking to Zach. He listens to you more than he does to me. I'll talk to O'Malley.''

"You'll talk to O'Malley?'' Angel was confused. "What good would that do?''

"You just do your half of the work—getting Zach to cooperate,'' Mrs. Martin said briskly. "I'll talk to O'Malley. I don't let anybody stand in my way when I want something for my sons.''

Angel caught her breath. Would paying for murder be something that Jeanne Martin would do in order to further her sons' interests?

"I'll drop Anna off with your sister-in-law,'' Mrs. Martin said. "She sometimes watches over Anna when I need…oh, dear, Maria won't be up to that, will she?''

"No, I don't think she will. She's taking some sedatives for the shock. And she's convinced that Zach murdered Tony.''

"Oh, dear, what a tragedy! Our two families seem to be destined for trouble. I'll take you up on that offer for baby-sitting. I'll catch the next commuter train. I can be downtown in half an hour."

"Meet me at the courthouse on Twenty-sixth and California. Felonies, third floor."

Chapter Fifteen

Twenty-sixth and California was a granite fortress in the middle of the burnt-out war zone of the south side of Chicago.

At eight-thirty in the morning, armed guards unlocked the doors and a line formed to pass through the metal detectors. Guns, knives and clubs were routinely confiscated.

Lawyers flashed their bar cards and were waved on through a separate entrance.

There were three elevators—one that never worked, one that worked occasionally and one that was always full and on another floor.

O'Malley and Angel waited for Mrs. Martin and Anna behind the metal detectors. When Mrs. Martin stepped out of the cab, wearing a dark aubergine silk crepe suit and matching hat, she held her arm protectively around Anna, who carried her Barbie doll.

O'Malley roused himself from a desultory conversation he was having with the chief of security.

"Mrs. Martin!" he called out. "Right this way."

Jeanne Martin had stood at the end of the line of people waiting to get through security, but when she saw O'Malley, she tugged at Anna's sleeve and led her daughter to the lawyer's entrance.

"Mr. O'Malley," she said, extending her hand. "Thank you for seeing me."

"My pleasure, Mrs. Martin," O'Malley said. "And good morning, Anna. That's a very pretty doll you have. Her dress looks like it matches yours."

"It's the other way around," Anna said, flashing an appreciative smile. "Mom had this dress made so that I would match Barbie. Hi, Angel. Where's Zach?"

The three other adults exchanged uncomfortable glances.

"Why don't we go this way and have a talk?" O'Malley suggested, leading the women to the private judge's elevator, which was being held open by a security guard.

"What floor, sir?" the guard asked.

"Top," O'Malley said.

The guard reached a hand inside the elevator to pop the button and nodded to each of the women as they entered the elevator.

"Better than dealing with the morning rush,"

O'Malley explained as they glided upward. "How was the ride in, Mrs. Martin?"

"Just fine, thank you."

The elevator doors opened to a lobby that was quiet and spare. O'Malley guided them past a receptionist, through a hallway of cubicles and into a large conference room with a black leather table.

METROPOLITAN CORRECTIONAL Center Inmate 143MCC was brought to Twenty-sixth and California in the van with five other men who had morning court appearances. His face was covered with sweat and stubble, his black hair fell onto his forehead and he couldn't push it back with his hands because they were cuffed tight against his back.

Though his eyes were not bloodshot, dark shadows showed his exhaustion. He had been granted the right to change into his street clothes for his arraignment, but his tie was missing, he had to use the center's slip-on sneakers because they had his shoes in lockup and he felt as wrinkled and worn as his jacket.

His van mates shuffled into the courtroom, but he was uncuffed and led through a back staircase. He rubbed his raw, red wrists.

"In there." The blue uniformed officer pointed a thumb at the conference room and took a guard position by the door.

Zach walked into the threshold. And saw the three women he loved more than anything in the world.

His mother pacing by the window. His sister, Anna, rocking quietly in a chair at the head of the conference table.

And Angel, coming into his arms, her scent so sweet with vanilla and talc that he felt ashamed of himself, knowing—as he did—that he carried the desperate acrid smell of the jail on his skin.

"Darling," she whispered. "How are you?"

"I'm all right, I think."

"We'll get you out of here," she promised, although both of them were wise enough to know she didn't have much control over that. "I love you."

She loved him. She believed in him. She held nothing back from him. No deception, no turning around, no reversals, no doubts. She loved him, and he needed that love right now so much that he didn't try to persuade her to go. He could live on her love for a long time. He buried his head in the crook of her neck, lifting her up off the floor so that he could feel her weight, slight as it was, and her substance.

If necessary, so he could remember...

"I'm all right," he said, coughing as he realized he hadn't actually spoken since he had been processed at the jail the previous night and his throat felt scratchy and worn. "How are you?"

"Tired. But okay."

"Happy reunion," O'Malley said, rising from a chair at the opposite end of the table. "We've got some serious business to talk about. Let go of him, Angel. Siddown, Zach."

Zach nearly charged. That was from nearly twelve hours of being caged in the jail with other inmates who regarded him as an agent of their sworn enemy, the law.

If he was reduced to this after twelve hours, he wondered at how he would feel after a week, a month, years....

He sat down at the conference table and squeezed his sister's hand. Angel sat on his other side and he entwined his fingers in hers. His mother kissed his hair and sat across from him.

"We have to get you out of here," she said.

"Easier said than done," O'Malley reminded them. "Murder is a capital offense."

"He didn't do it," Mrs. Martin said coldly.

"We know it was someone from the Martin family."

Jeanne sputtered and fell silent.

"Stop bugging my mom," Zach said. "Leave my mom, Angel and my sister out of this."

"Can't," O'Malley said.

"We both know the rules about interrogating a suspect," Zach said.

"I'm trying to do this for your own good,"

O'Malley said. "Because there's still a part of me—a small part, admittedly—that believes in you. Maybe it's just because you have Angel believing in you."

He pulled a black-and-white $8\frac{1}{2}$-by-11 photograph from an envelope. He shoved the picture across the table. "Anna, did you go to the bank recently?"

"Is the bank the place where they keep money?" Anna asked, scrunching up her nose.

Jeanne pulled a pair of tortoiseshell glasses out from her purse. "Can't you please leave my daughter out of this?" she asked.

"Do you know what's in your safety deposit box?" O'Malley asked.

Jeanne shrugged. "Some jewelry, the title to our house, a little bit of money."

"A lot of money. Who's a signatory?"

"Any person within our family with the last name Martin."

"Have you been to the bank lately?"

Zach took the picture from his mother. Angel leaned over his shoulder.

"No," Jeanne said. "Mr. O'Malley, forgive me for interrupting, but I thought this meeting was about getting Zach out of jail."

"O'Malley, what the hell is this all about?" Zach asked.

Anna raised her hand.

"Yes, Anna?" O'Malley said.

"I know what that is," she said, pointing to the picture in Zach's hand.

"What is it?"

"That's a picture from when I went to the bank to count our money," she said, pleased with herself for getting an answer right. "I went two times. Isabel took me."

"Isabel? You mean, Salvatore's fiancée?" Angel asked.

"Yes, we went to count money and I did such a good job, she took me out for ice cream," Anna said. "She's very pretty and she played Barbies with me. Did you know she's a model in Europe?"

"Dear God!" Jeanne exclaimed.

"When did you see her?" Angel asked, struggling to keep her voice calm so as not to scare Anna.

"It must have been when I dropped her off at Maria's," Jeanne said. "I've sometimes needed babysitting. Maria's been a great help to me. On the day of your parents' funeral she even sent her housekeeper over to take care of Anna. I didn't know she was making friends with Isabel, too."

"But, Anna, how did you get the key?" O'Malley asked impatiently.

"Key?"

"Yeah, every safety deposit box has a key."

"I didn't have a key," Anna said, eyes round with fear that she had done something wrong.

"You had to have used a key," O'Malley corrected.

"Back off my sister," Zach said.

"No, this is important," O'Malley said. "She's gotta tell us about the key."

"Not so important you have to badger her."

"Let him talk," Jeanne said. "Zach, if this gets you out of jail, I'm willing to do it."

"All right, Anna, dear," O'Malley said, clearly laboring over the soft endearment. "Don't be scared of me. I'm just a cantankerous old man."

"What does cantankerous mean?"

"An old jerk," O'Malley said.

Jeanne chuckled. O'Malley allowed himself a brief smile in her direction and then refocused on Anna.

"The box is locked. You can't open it without a key. How did you get a key? Did Isabel have it? Did someone give you the key?"

Anna shook her head at the myriad choices.

Zach sprung to his feet.

"Leave her alone!" he bellowed. "I've had enough from you, O'Malley. My sister has told you everything she can."

"It's all right, Zach, you can stop your steamin'. I've heard enough," O'Malley said. "I'll have Rocco, Isabel and Salvatore picked up today."

"Now you think they killed our parents?" Angel asked, the horrible possibilities swirling in her head.

"If that's true, then do you really think they killed Tony?"

"I think your brothers represent a possible homicide theory," O'Malley said. "It all fits together now. The younger brothers killed your parents and then Tony. Thinking they were going to run the business."

"That's ridiculous," Angel said. "Rocco's got a good heart and Salvatore doesn't like to be in charge of anything."

O'Malley shrugged.

"But then, who did you think took Anna to the safety deposit box?" Jeanne asked pointedly. "Before Anna told you it was Isabel?"

O'Malley ducked his head.

"I'm sorry, Mrs. Martin, I thought it might be you. Just because you are so devoted to taking care of Anna that we thought…"

"*You* thought," Angel corrected.

"All right, *I* thought it might be you."

"I want an apology right now," Jeanne said.

"Sorry," O'Malley said, as contrite as a schoolboy.

"I think you don't know what the hell you're doing," Zach said. "Am I free to go?"

"Yes, I'll call Processing and tell them to let you sign for your stuff." O'Malley looked up. "I'm glad to find out I was wrong about you." He glanced at Jeanne Martin. "And about you."

"You shouldn't have doubted me in the first place," Zach groused. "I've always played it straight."

"He's right," Jeanne agreed.

O'Malley held up his palms. As close to an apology as anyone would ever get from him.

"Where are you headed?"

"To get the one man you're too scared to touch," Zach said.

"I said we're bringing in Rocco and Salvatore. Isabel, too. And Maria, for questioning, if she's up to it."

"I'm not talking about them."

"If you're talking about your brother, I want one thing perfectly clear. If you know where he is, you should be helping me bring him in for questioning, too."

"I don't know where he is and that's not who I'm talking about."

O'Malley blanched.

Zach calmly kissed his mother's cheek, startling her, and leaned over to tousle Anna's hair. "Don't let the bad man scare you."

"Zach, don't go," his mother cried.

"Zach, wherever you're going, I'm going, too," Angel warned, scrambling to her feet.

Zach looked back from the doorway.

"No, Angel, you take Anna with you," he said. "Right, Mother? She needs my protection. Now more than ever."

Jeanne took a deep breath.

"You're right. Anna, stay with Angel."

"Kill a few hours and then meet me at the airport at noon," Zach directed. "This time we'll leave together. All three of us."

"I'm going with you?" Anna asked excitedly. "I've never taken an airplane ride."

"Well, you're going to today," Zach said. "But first, I have to take care of a few things."

"Zach, I'm going with you," Angel insisted. "If you're planning some kind of showdown with my brothers, I want to be there."

He shook his head. "Angel, she needs your protection now," he said. "I'm asking you to do it."

"You're ordering me and it's not going to work."

"Angel, I'm not ordering you around, I'm asking for your help."

Angel looked at Anna, who sat with wide-eyed anticipation.

"Please," he added.

"All right, but we'll go out of here together," she said.

"Mom, is it okay if I go with them?" Anna asked.

Jeanne wiped away tears from her cheeks. "Yes,

darling,'' she said, struggling to compose herself. ''Zach and Angel will take care of you. You're going to have a great time on the airplane.''

''Then why are you crying?''

''Because I love you very much.''

''I love you, too, Mom,'' Anna said, and got up to give her mother a hug. ''Goodbye, Mr. O'Malley.''

O'Malley glanced at Zach and then tousled Anna's hair.

''Goodbye, Anna. And goodbye, Barbie. Have a nice plane ride. And, Zach?''

''What?''

''Don't take the law into your own hands. Just say what you have to say and get out.''

''I think that's advice you should have followed yourself,'' Zach said. ''Many years ago, O'Malley, many years ago.''

Chapter Sixteen

He walked down the hallway swiftly, feeling rather than seeing Angel and Anna struggling to keep up. He didn't like pushing them, but he knew that he didn't have a lot of time.

"Zach, Zach, what's going on?" Angel demanded. "I don't understand what's going on."

Seeing the line at the elevator bank, he shoved open the door to the inside fire escape, disengaged the alarm and took the stairs two at a time. The fire escape was cool, a relief after the pressed-in heat of the rest of the building. The concrete walls were painted in a muted industrial gray.

"Zach, you have to tell me what's going on or I'm stopping right now," she said.

"As long as you keep Anna out of trouble, that'd be fine with me."

He walked halfway down the landing to the next and then realized that Anna and Angel hadn't moved.

He looked up the stairs. Angel stood at the top of the landing above him.

"Zach, you always act as if I'm so fragile and in need of protection," Angel said. "Like you're my protector, my guardian angel."

"You do need protection," he said, adding for the sake of her pride, "Sometimes."

"But not always."

"Hey, are we having a domestic dispute? Because this isn't the kind of thing I have time for today. There's a murderer loose, O'Malley's too scared to take him in and God only knows which one of your family is going to die next. If we live through the day, I'd be happy to argue with you later."

She didn't budge.

"Fine. You can stay here. In the stairwell. It's nice and cool. Just make sure that you get to the airport by noon. With Anna."

He walked down two more steps before her voice stopped him cold.

"It's just like ten years ago."

"How?"

"You're protecting me from something," she said, and he nodded. "But you're not giving me enough information so that I can even know what I should be afraid of. And you're not letting me help you."

Anna, bored and tired, sat down on the top step next to Angel's legs.

"Zach, how am I supposed to protect Anna if I don't even know what I'm protecting her from?"

Zach hung his head, running through a dozen options with the precision of a high-speed computer. He liked to work alone. He didn't trust easily. He felt responsible for the people he loved. He was a man who had trouble with thinking of Angel as a woman with her own mind.

"All right, you two are coming with me," he conceded, knowing as the words left his mouth that he wasn't being any less autocratic by letting them tag along. "I'll explain what I can along the way. But when I tell you I want to do something alone or if I tell you to do something, you have to respect that. Understand?"

Anna nodded because she always did.

Angel gave him a smile that made him feel like a goof for wanting that smile so much.

"Okay," she said. "But that kind of deal's off after today. I'm not living the rest of my life like some kind of wench out of the sixteenth century."

"After today, I don't care how much trouble you are. Let's get moving," he ordered. "We're doing what we have to do and then we're getting out of this city."

THE PROCESSING DESK CLERK handed him a plastic zip bag. Inside were his tie, his shoes and shoelaces, all of which were routinely confiscated from prisoners so that they were not used as weapons. Also inside was his wallet—his money and credit cards intact.

"Where's my gun?" he asked, running his shoelaces through. Angel worked on the other shoe.

The uniformed desk clerk looked up from her fashion magazine with an I-was-not-put-on-this-earth-to-help-you snarl.

"We keep the weapons."

"I have a license to carry," Zach replied evenly, pulling his ID from his wallet. "I had a Walther PPK, a shoulder holster and a second clip of ammunition."

She shook her head. "We keep the weapons."

"I want mine back," he said, shoving the ID across the desk. "I'm an assistant district attorney. I'm entitled to my gun."

She looked at the ID. Unimpressed. She shoved a quarter across the counter.

"You can call the district attorney's office and take it up with them," she said. "But I got my orders. You don't get your weapon back. Nobody does. Can I help you, sir?"

She strained her neck, as if the next man in line were of great interest to her.

"Zach, give it up," Angel said. She held up his shoe. "Why don't we get out of here?"

Zach looked once at the quarter and again at the clerk and calculated the headache factor involved in getting his gun back.

"All right, we're out of here," he said. "Do you have my car?"

Angel held up the keys. He reached, but she snatched her hand away.

"I'll drive," she said.

He was about to tell her how it would be. And then he smiled. Let her drive, he thought. It would give him a moment to rest and it would make her feel, just for a moment, as if she were in charge. Because later he might have to tell her to do things his way. And he might not have the time to argue.

"First stop, my apartment," he said. "Come on, Anna."

UPSTAIRS, IN THE penthouse conference room, Jeanne Martin took in the panoramic view of Chicago. To the north were the glamorous Gold Coast town homes, to the south the University of Chicago and its Gothic buildings. To the west were the projects, hulls of good intentions now burnt out by gang wars.

Beyond the projects, nearly clouded over by the exhaust mist of morning traffic, was Bridgeport, where it all began for her.

Where too many dreams had died.

Too many foolish choices had been made.

Choices she had had to live with for her whole life.

Where had all the years gone?

She thought about Guy. Always a problem child, maybe because he was her first and she had been so lacking in confidence. More likely, he was simply made that way. Pugnacious, loud, with more physical energy than most. Like his father. But his legal father wasn't like that.

There had always been an uneasy fit between Guy, Sr., and Jr. But Guy, Sr., had been so blinded by pride and by the contrast between his two sons and his daughter Anna that he had overlooked every niggling doubt.

Until a few months ago.

What had made it change was knowing instead of simply suspecting. Somehow he had known.

Her husband had confused poor young Guy, suddenly freezing him out of a relationship that had been the younger man's life. Suddenly father didn't want long-into-the-night conversations with son. Suddenly, Guy, Jr., wasn't the man he wanted for business talks and beach walks. Suddenly, Guy, Sr., didn't love his son anymore.

Because he knew.

And then an insidious attention had been focused on Zach.

"I'm sorry, Jeanne," O'Malley said, walking up behind her. He stood without embracing her. She would not have pushed away his arms.

"I know you are."

"I've screwed up so many things and now I've lost…we've lost…"

"Please, don't."

"I should have listened to you. Thirty-eight years ago, I should have listened to you. I should have gotten down on my hands and knees and begged you to marry me in the same sentence as I asked for your forgiveness. But I didn't. And we've had to live with that stupidity."

"It could still turn out all right. Do we know where Guy is?"

"No, but I'm not very hopeful."

She looked down at the floor.

He was right. He was absolutely right.

"If he's still alive, if he's out there, I swear to you, Jeanne, I'll do my best."

She turned around.

He was crying, his face wet with tears that he made no effort to hide.

"I'm so sorry, Jeanne. What I should have done was claim him as my own a long, long time ago."

Jeanne shook her head grimly. "No, that wouldn't have saved him."

SITTING IN THE LIVING room of his apartment, Zach checked and loaded his automatic. The one he kept in the drawer of his desk. Just in case. He heard the knock on the door. He flicked the safety.

"If your name isn't Angel, you'd better leave," he said, and aimed.

When he saw Angel, he put the gun down on the glass coffee table.

Dammit, she smelled so clean and pure even after a night that felt as long as a year. Her hair was as shiny as a gold piece. And her pale blue eyes—Zach could forget himself, forget everything, every horrible thing, in those eyes. He chuckled. Even her bubble gum pink lip gloss looked right.

He had changed into a pair of jeans and a clean shirt, brushed his grimy teeth and had wasted five minutes unsuccessfully looking for his razor.

"I thought I told you to stay in the car," he said, rubbing his chin.

"You were taking a long time."

"Where's Anna?"

"She's in the back seat."

"You shouldn't have left her alone."

"Zach, you spent the whole ride over with your eyes closed," Angel said. "I can understand that you needed some rest. And I can also understand that this isn't the sort of thing we should talk about in front of Anna. But you need to tell me…"

"Angel, just trust me. I love you."

With a staccato beat, the mirror over the fireplace shattered into a million pieces. Glass rained upon the living room floor.

"Angel!"

He shoved her down to the floor. A shadow passed across the balcony. Zach grabbed his gun from the holster on the floor. Rolling onto his back, he kicked the front door open. Bullets flew over his head, hammering the opposite wall. As the door swung back, the bullets ripped the heavy oak off its hinges and sent it flying down the stairwell.

"Angel, get out of here!" Zach shouted. "Crawl out. I'll cover you. Get to the car and get Anna the hell out of here!"

He fired off several rounds to shield her escape. But Angel couldn't move, rooted to the floor with fear or perhaps a sense of loyalty that wouldn't let her leave him in danger.

Suddenly the guns fell silent.

A silence broken only by a deep, guttural moan.

"Oh, man, you got me."

Zach walked out onto the balcony. Angel cautiously stood.

"Dear God!"

Angel leapt to Zach's side and stared at the collapsed assailant.

At first, she didn't recognize him, and then, when

she did, she fell to her knees. Zach yanked off his shirt and knelt down to staunch the blood from a gaping abdominal wound his own bullets had wrought.

"Guy…how badly are you hurt?" Zach begged.

In the glow of sunlight filtering through the green maple leaves, Guy's face was bleached and bloated.

"It's over Zach. I'm dead."

"No, Guy, no, it's not like that," Zach said. "You took a hit the day before yesterday. This is just another one. We'll get a doctor."

But one glance at the soaked shirt was the horrible confirmation. Reaching under the bandages the doctor had put on him just the day before, Angel's fingers felt the life pulse of his brother weaken and ebb.

"It's you or me," Guy said. "If I had the strength to lift this hand right now, I'd grab my gun and take you down, brother."

"Why?" Angel was shocked. "He's always been a good brother to you."

"Dog-eat-dog world. Zach's trying to take over the two families," Guy whispered, staring defiantly at his brother. "And word on the street is that you've already gotten satisfaction on a contract for my life."

"No, Guy."

"Let me finish. Taking me out so that you can take over. Well, I was frightened at first, but then I knew I wouldn't go down without a fight. The Martin family's mine, Zach. You weren't there to learn the business. I was. I deserve it. It's mine. I worked for it.''

"None of this is true!" Zach protested. "Guy, I've always loved you. We've had our disagreements, but I would never put out a contract on you and I don't want any part of the family business. That's the truth."

"Well, the truth doesn't matter now, does it?" Guy said wryly, touching a weak finger to the thin bubbles of blood that formed on his mouth.

"The truth always matters."

"And what is the truth? Only that you're probably better suited. You're stronger, independent, a clear thinker, courageous. Me? Aw, who am I fooling? Sometimes I'd rather have never been..." He coughed up black mucous that dribbled down his pale shirt. "Have never been who I am..."

"Guy, who told you this about Zach?" Angel begged.

He looked as if he might answer, but then he arched his back, holding out his fingers to Zach, who took them in his sure grip, and, with a gasp, Guy Martin died.

His eyes dulled. His stare hardened. His mouth fell slack.

Zach and Angel looked at each other.

Angel swallowed her horror and revulsion.

"We would never have had a chance to get him

an ambulance," she reassured, soothing the damp tendrils of hair on Guy's pale forehead. "There was nothing you could have done."

"I could have not fired," Zach said, shaking his head. "Angel, I killed my own brother."

"You didn't know," Angel said. "He had come to kill you. Zach, he must have been the one who murdered my parents. And Tony."

"No, he wasn't," Zach cut her off. "I know what you're thinking, Angel, but Guy wasn't like that. He didn't order your parents killed and he didn't have anything to do with Tony. He was dumb and he was mean sometimes—Lord forgive me for thinking that—but he was never cold-blooded."

"Who would tell him that you have a contract out on him?"

He pressed Guy's eyelids shut and murmured a quick but solemn prayer. When he looked up into Angel's eyes, his face was grim and hard.

"Get Anna and drive away," he ordered. He stood and picked his shoulder holster from the floor. "Call the police in half an hour from a pay phone. Tell them there's a body here and go to the airport. I'll meet you at Terminal B, by the luggage carousel. If I'm not there by noon, get on a plane. Go anywhere in the world. But don't come back."

"You don't think you're coming with me, do you?"

He picked up several bullet casings and headed down the hall into the bathroom.

"I'm not sure," he called back, over the roar of the water rushing into the sink.

Angel eased herself out from under Guy's limp weight. She found Zach as he came out of the bathroom, wiping the traces of blood from his hands.

He brusquely passed her and snagged a clean shirt from the top dresser drawer.

Then he checked and reloaded his gun and strapped on his shoulder holster.

"We're going with you," Angel said. "Wherever you're headed."

"No way." He shook his head, shoving the desk drawer closed. "This is a man's job."

One look at his steel gray eyes persuaded her that chiding his sexism wasn't an option.

He brushed past her and she followed him into the living room. He put on his jacket, stared long and hard at the balcony, the cool early summer wind wafting the light curtains like the hems of angels' gowns. The living room floor was covered with broken glass and splattered blood; his brother's body lay quietly on the edge of the glass doors to the balcony.

"I swear to you, Guy," he whispered as Angel stood behind him. "I swear to you, Guy, I will not let him get away with this."

"What do you mean 'him'?" Angel cried.

But he had already swept out of the apartment.

Angel grabbed her purse and followed him down the stairs. An old woman in the apartment across the hall opened her door, peered out and then slammed her door shut.

"I'm going with you!" Angel repeated.

At the bottom of the stairs, he glanced back at her.

"Zach, I'm not being left behind!"

From the distance, they could hear a police siren. Another neighbor's door opened and then abruptly closed. They both knew they didn't have a lot of time.

"They'll take me in," she observed. "Even if they don't think I'm to blame, they'll hold me. Think what they'll do to Anna. O'Malley would be just the kind to rip the head off the Barbie doll and make Anna talk."

He stared out at the sidewalk, the reflection of a squad car's cherry lights dappling the dark underbellies of the leaves.

"Come on!"

He held the glass security door for her and they ran up the block to his Camaro.

"What's going on?" Anna asked.

"Nothing, Anna," Zach said. "Did you see Guy around here?"

"No, was he supposed to be here?"

"No, honey, just wondering."

With a shared glance, Angel and Zach agreed not

to say anything to her about Guy's fate. There would be time enough for that later.

"Where are we going?" Angel asked as he started the engine.

"Where it all began," he said, glancing in the rearview mirror as he eased the car out of its parking slot. A police car screeched to a halt in back of them, but Zach drove slow and sure to avoid undue attention.

They weren't there when O'Malley arrived, sweeping into the apartment with a drab raincoat and the smell of tobacco.

They weren't there when O'Malley saw Guy's body, when he stumbled and complained to the officer who helped him to his feet that his damn blood pressure pills were giving him trouble.

They weren't there when he reached down to touch the cool, dry skin of Guy's face.

They weren't there when O'Malley walked out to the edge of the balcony and closed his eyes against the brash sunlight.

It only lasted a moment, his dizzy spell. Then he gruffly demanded a cell phone and called his office.

"Has she left yet? No? Well, put her on the phone," he said. "Jeanne? I've got something to tell you. Sit down, please."

Chapter Seventeen

The red Camaro pulled onto Lake Shore Drive, passing the towering luxury lakeside apartment buildings and the vast greenery of Lincoln Park.

The air was scented with pine and the freshwater breeze off Lake Michigan. The North Avenue beach was packed, even though it was a weekday.

Zach gripped the covered steering wheel with his left hand and stared impassively at the traffic.

His right hand clung to Angel's, and sometimes, as his mind wandered to what he was about to do, he would tighten his fingers until she winced. Then he would back off and remind himself to stay focused.

On these few precious minutes with Angel.

Because he had no idea what was coming next, but he knew it wouldn't be good.

In twenty silent minutes, he passed the curving ravines of Glencoe's outer limits. The sun scattered jewellike sparkles across the lake's waves and through the maple and birch branches.

He pulled up the gravel-covered circular driveway to his parents' home and raked a tired hand through his hair.

"What are you going to do?" she asked, her face etched with tension.

He didn't answer the question.

"Go upstairs and pack up anything Anna wants to take with her. Try to make it carry-on because I don't want to waste time at check-in. Trust me, Angel, please trust me. I'm not ordering you around, I'm desperate for your help."

She looked at him thoughtfully and then nodded.

"Anna, come on, honey. We're going to pack up some stuff for the plane ride."

"Don't go into the conservatory," he warned. "I have business to take care of."

ZACH STRODE INTO the octagonal conservatory filled with the purple and white orchids that were his father's passion.

The air was sweet—too sweet—and sticky with the scent of orchids. The glass walls were foggy with early-morning condensation. Palm leaf and lemon grass reached to the tin ceiling. Terrazzo glistened beneath Zach's blood-splattered shoes. Water gurgled from a fountain of cherubs and brilliant orange goldfish wavered near the mossy bottom.

Zach used rudimentary sign language to tell Inga to clear out. Which, mercifully, she did—padding out silently in her crepe shoes.

His father's wheelchair faced the bluff overlooking the lake.

Recovering from a violent coughing fit, Guy Martin, Sr., barely inclined his head toward his younger son.

"I was wondering when you would come," he wheezed.

"You're a monster," Zach said, sitting on the granite bench in front of his father.

"Maybe I am," his father conceded with a labored lift of his shoulders. "But you always see things as so very black-and-white."

Zach's voice dropped to a murderous calm. "There is no gray on this one. You arranged the deaths of your best friend and his wife."

"He wasn't my best friend."

"He was your only friend. You arranged the death of his son. You set up your eldest son to be killed by his younger brother—that's me—but I bet you would have settled for vice versa."

His father propped himself up on one elbow and craned his neck forward to confirm the news.

"Guy is dead?"

"By my own hand."

"Dear God," he said with only a touch of squeamishness. "But you survived."

"Yes."

"You should know I wouldn't have settled for vice versa."

Zach recoiled. "You're a monster. You fed Guy that talk about me putting out a contract on him, didn't you?"

"So I did. If you were a real man, it might have been true."

"And you arranged for the death of your friend."

His father shook his head. "Tony, Sr., was no friend of mine," he corrected. "He would have ordered a hit on me if he thought it would be good for his business."

"His wife...?"

"Antoinette I feel bad about," Guy conceded. "She was a good woman. An innocent woman. Antoinette's death was a mistake. Not my mistake, you understand. The gun I hired admitted a mistake, but said it was difficult to get a clear shot. She usually came out of the car last, after her husband. It was a habit that she should have kept."

"Who is Marcus Jones?"

"I have no clue."

"The hit man. I heard a tape of him."

"Must have been Rocco doing one of his famous impersonations," Guy said.

"Why would he do that?"

"Tony would tell him to do it. Rocco is a man who likes to be told what to do."

"Who was the hit man?"

His father chuckled. "The hit man was a woman."

"A woman?"

"I'm a great believer in equal opportunity. She came very well recommended. Absolute pro. And she's got a great rear."

Zach didn't rise to the bait.

"All right, what about Tony, Jr.? Was that done by your pro?"

"I didn't have anything to do with that. I didn't kill him and I didn't pay to have him done."

"I don't believe you."

His father shrugged. "It's part of an everyday struggle. A business struggle."

"And Guy?"

"Him I don't care about."

"You don't care about your own son?"

His father coughed and Zach reflexively fixed him a glass of water. Recovering, his father muttered a curse. "He wasn't my son," Guy Martin said, finding a place for his glass on the tray table crowded with prescription bottles, paperbacks and tissues. "You're my only son. And this, all of this," he crowed, gesturing to the lake that stretched out before them. "This, my son, is your birthright."

"Guy isn't your son?" Zach demanded.

Guy, Sr., squeezed a breath from the inhalator. "No," he grunted.

"Not my brother?"

Guy sucked in more medicine. He shook his head.

"Half brother?" Zach guessed.

Guy, Sr., dropped the inhalator and took several labored breaths before looking at his son. "Yes, but not of my blood. Considering you're my child, you're awfully dense."

Zach ignored the insult. "How did it happen?"

"Your mother's a tramp."

"Try better language."

"Have it your way. Your mother dated both of us, me and Sciopelli. They broke up abruptly. I thought I had triumphed by winning her from him. We married immediately, me congratulating myself on my victory at love."

"It sounds more like war than love."

"It was a little of both. Anyway, I didn't pay too much attention to the exact date of Guy's arrival—he was early but your mother and I had been intimate. I didn't even imagine that she could have betrayed me. Times were good and we made money, all of us—Tony made sure to put a lot of money into my pockets. I thought he was doing it because we were friends.''

''What changed?''

''It all changed when the shopping mall contract with the Winnetka Village trustees came up, and I found out the horrible truth.''

''What truth?''

His father wheezed uncomfortably and reached for the inhalator.

''Guy had been screwing up on a lot of jobs and I was too sick to handle the business. When the shopping mall came up, Tony, Jr., fought hard to have the Martin company cut out of the deal. Even out of the very lucrative trucking operation. The empty truck operations.''

''Drugs?''

''Don't be so prissy. We simply used trucks that had been used to cart materials for shipping other items that weren't government approved. Let's not have the drug argument again, all right?''

''Fine. Just tell me—then what?''

''Then Tony, Sr., explained to Tony, Jr., that Guy was 'protected' and that Guy would always work Sciopelli jobs, would always be taken care of. As family. He didn't come right out and say he was Guy's father, but the message was there. Tony, Jr., went ballistic and came to me with the truth.''

He started to cough.

Zach handed him a tissue.

"Thanks. I was stunned and didn't believe it at first. But I thought about it and realized it must be so. The poor kid felt as betrayed as I did."

Zach had trouble thinking of Tony, Jr., as a "poor kid." He had always seemed older than his years. On the other hand, he hadn't deserved to die. Or had he?

"Did you talk this over with Mother?"

His father eyed him coldly. "I could have talked to her a lot better if I didn't always have you looking over my shoulder."

"You won't raise a hand to her—or let anyone else," Zach said. "That's always been the deal. It doesn't change now. Even now."

"Always defending her. Well, it doesn't matter. I stopped paying the tab for Anna's occupational therapy to put the squeeze on her."

"That's unfair."

"It doesn't violate our agreement—that I not lay a hand on either of them."

"Did you go back to paying?"

"Yes, after your mother admitted last month Guy wasn't mine—that was enough proof for me that Tony, Sr., had been duping me all those years."

Zach did little to hide his revulsion.

"And you had your friend killed because of something that happened over thirty-five years ago?"

"He betrayed us. All of us. Tony and I agreed to have his father killed. Tony wasn't any happier about the situation than I was," Guy Martin protested.

"But you don't kill a man for that."

"Tony, Sr.? He deserved it." His father snorted. "The man foisted upon me a son I had raised as my own because he didn't want to marry Jeanne. From Tony, Jr.'s perspective he was saddling the Sciopelli business with his spawn. I took care of paying for the hit. Little Tony took care that no suspicion or retribution would come to me."

"Then why'd you kill Tony, Jr.?"

"Tony, Jr.?" his father asked, sucking a deep breath from the inhalator. "Little Tony didn't know I had a side deal."

UPSTAIRS, ANGEL HELD up a Skipper doll.

"I think we can fit in three more dolls," she said to Anna. "Do you want to take Skipper or do you want to leave her behind?"

Anna sat on the bed playing with her sneaker's pink laces. "I don't know," she said sullenly.

Angel sat down on the bed.

"Maybe you don't want to go with me and Zach?"

"I don't know."

"Anna, are you scared about going?"

Anna twisted her mouth. "I don't know," she repeated. She looked up. "Hi, Maria."

Angel whirled.

Maria stood in the doorway. She wore a floral print sundress and a pair of espadrilles. Her hair was pulled back in a ponytail and she looked startling refreshed considering her husband had been brutally murdered the night before.

Angel was so stunned by the contrast between the Maria who had been sobbing hysterically at the station house and the one standing before her now that she nearly missed the gun.

Held in Maria's perfectly manicured fingers.

"Maria, if this is about Tony," she said, moving away from Anna, "I didn't have anything to do with it and neither did Zach."

"Ha, you're a riot." Maria laughed mirthlessly. "You always were such a straight arrow. Such a straight arrow. Worrying about the little widow."

"How are you feeling?" Angel said, sliding down the bed so that if Maria intended on shooting her, Anna would not get hurt. But Maria had other plans. She jerked the gun suddenly. "Get up off the bed—you're not taking Skipper or any other Barbies anywhere. Bring the retard, too."

"What did she call me?" Anna asked as she followed Angel.

"Nothing, Anna," Angel said, putting her arm around Anna. "Just come along."

By the butt of her gun, Maria escorted Angel and Anna down the stairs to the Martin front hall. Rocco stood waiting.

"Darling," he said to Maria, kissing her offered cheek. "I'll take over from here."

He took the gun from Maria and trained it on Angel and Anna. Maria stood behind him, smiling triumphantly.

"You should have left when you had the chance," Rocco told Angel.

"They'll be going soon enough," Maria said. "Let's have our little chat with Mr. Martin."

ZACH ROSE to his feet the moment Angel entered the room. She tugged behind her Anna, who was quietly crying and quivering with fright. As Maria and Rocco stepped behind them, Zach grimaced. His eyes met Angel's and he was surprised she was not more frightened.

Perhaps she didn't know what the possibilities were.

Or perhaps she had learned his trait of greatest calm in the face of greatest danger.

He patted the seat next to him and Anna sat down, latching her arms around his waist.

"It's all right, little pumpkin," he soothed, not believing his words.

Angel sat on his other side. She put her head on his shoulder.

"I'm sorry," she said. "I should have been watching for trouble."

"Don't worry, we'll think of a way to get out of this one," Zach said.

Flopping one leg over the arm of the chintz-upholstered love seat against the window, Maria snapped her gum. "All right, old man, it's time to divvy up," she said. "Rocco, baby, sit down next to me."

In the doorway, Rocco rubbed his thick, sunburned neck. "No, I want to keep an eye out."

"For what?"

"I dunno."

Maria glanced at Angel. "Didn't know about me and Rocco, did you?"

"No," Angel admitted.

"He was in my grade all the way through school," Maria said. "We always loved each other, right, Rocco?"

"That's no reason to kill a man," Angel said.

"It wasn't quite like that. Tony thought he had wooed me away from him, but like I said at dinner night before last, first loves always win out. Rocco, darling, you don't need to stand watch. There's nobody to be afraid of.''

Rocco sat down next to Maria, keeping one hand firmly on his gun while Maria entwined her fingers around his other.

"Zach, put your piece down on the floor," he said.

"How did you know?" Zach asked.

"I'm not as dumb as I look."

Zach pulled his gun out of his holster and put it down on the cool terrazzo floor.

"Rocco, did you know your brother killed your parents?"

"I found out about it when he asked me to do the tape," Rocco said. "You know, the one with Marcus Jones on it. Then I knew. It was bad enough he took my woman. But he killed my parents. It made me mad. Real mad. It wasn't all that hard to take care of the car."

"I knew all along," Maria said. "I tried to persuade Rocco that Tony, Jr., was like that, but he didn't want to believe me."

"How long have you and Maria been…back together?" Angel asked.

"None of your business," Maria snapped. "This isn't question and answer time. This is money time."

"Money time?" Zach asked.

"Yeah, let's talk money, Mr. Martin," Maria said. "We both got stuff on each other. Tony, Jr., and the parents. We all know enough to put us all away for a long time.''

Rocco winced at the mention of his family.

"It's okay, darling," Maria said. "Tony was going to cut ·you out anyway, baby. But that's been taken care of. I won't let you down. Now, Mr. Martin, we have only one problem—your son, Guy, Jr.''

"He's already been taken care of," the elder Martin said calmly.

"Really?" Maria asked. She glanced over at Zach, noting his stricken face. "How very efficient. He was the cause of a lot of trouble. You can tell me all about it later. For now, let's get down to business. Zach, are you familiar with the terms?''

Angel bristled. He saw a flicker of movement in the trees and made a quick calculation.

"I'm willing to talk business, but can't we leave Anna out of this?" Zach asked Maria. "She'll get bored, uncooperative and she'll keep this from being a productive meeting.''

"I guess it's okay," Maria said cautiously.

"Get her out of here," Mr. Martin agreed.

"Anna, go upstairs," Zach said. "Play with your Barbies. Remember the costume I bought for your Ken doll? The blue one? I don't think you've ever put it on him. Why don't you try it?''

"This is not the time to be talking about doll fashions," Maria said.

"I'm just trying to get her situated so she won't bother us, right, Anna?"

"Right," Anna said. "I love you, Zach."

"I love you, too, honey," he said, kissing her. When Anna closed the door behind him, he turned to Maria and Rocco. "All right, let's talk business. Bring me up to speed on the terms."

"Are you nuts?" Angel whispered urgently.

"My Angel," he said to the others. "Such a worrywart."

He leaned over to her, kissing her lightly behind the ear. "Trust me," he whispered. "I'm giving you an order. Please, go down on the count of three. This time no questions." He sat up straight.

"Now, Maria, why don't you explain the business terms again?"

Maria smiled and pulled a cigarette out of the box on the glass occasional table.

"Thanks, honey," she said when Rocco lit it for her. For an instant, Zach thought the movement in the trees was an optical illusion created by the thick, confident stream of smoke she blew into the air.

"Go on, Maria," he said.

"Zach, as you know, your father wanted to position you to take over the Martin end of the business. He assumed, I suppose correctly because you're here, that you would eventually be persuaded that O'Malley's a jerk, that you have no future in the

D.A.'s office and that the only way to play ball in this town is to play with us. We're dividing this city up."

"One, I'm not surprised," Zach said, keeping an eye on the flickering trees outside the conservatory window. He loosened his arm from behind Angel so that she would have unrestricted movement. "Two, I'm grateful that my father would do so much for me."

"Glad you feel that way," Mr. Martin said, pondering an array of prescription bottles on the tray. "Knew you'd come around."

"Is there more?" Rocco grunted.

"Yeah," Zach said as Isabel came out of the trees into the clearing. She carried an automatic rifle with a laser clip attached for accuracy. "There's three."

He shoved down hard on the back of Angel just as she hit the ground. He grabbed for his gun, but it skittered away in a hail of glass shards. Maria screamed.

Rocco fell to the floor, his face frozen in surprise, the only sign of his distress being a red exit wound on his forehead.

The second round took down Maria. Her body jerked and slumped beside Rocco.

Mr. Martin kept his eyes closed throughout the attack, a spasm on his crepelike lids his only concession to danger.

Zach recovered his gun and, crouching behind the love seat, searched for any sign of Isabel.

"She's long gone," Mr. Martin advised calmly, popping a sedative into his mouth. He downed it with a glass of water. "I told you she was good. Professional, too. Came with excellent references."

Zach looked across the bloodied conservatory floor to the two bodies. Rocco jerked once, twice and then stilled.

"Why the hell did you do that?"

"Because I'm dying and I want to make sure that my family gets what it deserves," Mr. Martin said, smacking his lips as his pills hit his stomach.

"You've destroyed your family."

He gave Zach a clear-eyed gaze. "I only have one family member."

"No, no, you have a whole family," Zach corrected. "People who have relied on you, taken care of you, loved you all your life."

"I have a wife who foisted another man's child on me, a daughter who's going to play with Barbie dolls for the rest of her life, a son who was an idiot and not mine anyway, and then there's you. As far as I'm concerned, you're the last of my family. And there's a delicious irony about it all."

"What's that?"

"When you marry her, I'll have bested every one of them," Mr. Martin mused.

Zach helped Angel to her feet.

"Me?" Angel asked.

"Yeah, you. You're the key to it all."

"I'm not going into the business," Zach said.

"The business will come to you," his father countered. "Remember what happened when you tried to get a job as a lawyer? Everyone wanted you, because they thought a chunk of Martin and Sciopelli business came with. The law firms were fighting one another for a chance to hire you."

"I wouldn't have done your dirty work."

"It won't matter. Nothing you do will mess with my plans. Chicago is a surprisingly small town—everyone knows what and where you come from and nobody's going to forget. So thank me or don't thank me. Hate me or not. One day you will have to take it. Starting today, actually. I'll just be able to die knowing this was passed on—to my bloodline, not his."

It was then that they heard the sirens.

"Anna!" Angel said. "She's coming down the stairs."

Angel went to make sure that Anna wouldn't come into the conservatory and see the carnage.

"You are not my father any longer," Zach said with great effort but also a great sense of relief. He realized it had been a weight sitting heavily upon him.

"You are always my son," Guy, Sr., responded calmly. "You'll have to run pretty far to escape from the name Martin. Or the name Sciopelli. Those two names will be linked forever. That is, if you give in to your desire for her."

He began to cough, heave and wheeze.

But instead of bringing him water or flipping on the oxygen tank, Zach left him.

"Inga!" he yelled for the nurse, knowing that she could take care of things more competently if less personally than he could. He felt so revolted he thought he might throw up, but then he calmed himself, knowing that he had to be strong just a little longer.

Anna stood in the doorway with her round red Barbie suitcase. "Did I do a good job calling the police?" she asked.

"You did wonderful, kid," Zach said, kissing her forehead.

He steadied Angel, who was beginning to feel the effects of shock. She was trembling and her skin was cool—he needed to get them both out of here.

"Anna, you called 911?" Angel asked, leaning against Zach for support.

"Yes, it's a special code Zach and I set up," Anna said proudly. "The special outfit for Ken is the blue policeman's outfit. And that meant I was supposed to get the police."

"That's phenomenal."

"I might be slow," Anna said solemnly. "Maybe I'm even a retard like Maria said, but I can still do good things."

"You did a very good thing," Angel said, hugging the young woman.

Zach looked up the stairs.

"Where's Inga?"

"In her room."

"Fine, we'll leave her. The police will take twenty minutes just to figure out she can't speak English. And my father won't talk to them."

"Zach, aren't we going to wait for the police?" Angel asked.

"No, Angel. My father is right about one thing. The Martin and Sciopelli names are tough to shake," he said. "But we're going to do it. Come on, we're clearing out."

"We're leaving forever?"

He nodded.

"Zach, this is what I've always wanted."

He let his hair fall in front of his face so that she couldn't see his anguished expression. After he pulled the Camaro out into the street, they turned onto busy Green Bay Road just seconds before two Glencoe squad cars pulled up to the driveway.

Chapter Eighteen

The ticket agent typed furiously for several moments, bit her lip as she studied the screen in front of her and at last shook her head.

"I'm sorry, sir, we don't have two seats on the flight to San Salvador," she said. "But I can put one of you on the flight and then see if I can book one other seat for the next day's flight. That's the best I can do for two passengers."

"We aren't two passengers and we don't need two seats," Angel said. "We need three seats. Don't we, Zach?"

He looked away. The man in line behind Angel muttered to his wife that the service was slow at this airline.

"Well, it doesn't matter," the ticket agent said. "We don't have three seats, either. The flights to San Salvador are usually booked solid. Now, ma'am, is there anything else I can do for you? Because there's a great many other people in line.''

She smiled at the man standing behind Angel, but Zach held his ground.

''What about the twelve-thirty to Guatemala?'' he asked.

''I can check again, sir,'' the agent said with limited patience. ''But thirty seconds ago, when you last asked, the flight was booked.''

''I forgot we tried Guatemala. Try Fiji.''

''Checking, sir. Do you just need two seats?''

''Just two,'' he confirmed.

''Zach, why are we buying just two tickets?'' Angel demanded. ''Are we planning on leaving Anna here?''

They both glanced over at Anna, who was seated on a blue vinyl bench by the elevators. She clutched her Barbie suitcase to her chest and quietly rocked. Back and forth. Back and forth. Singing a nursery rhyme to herself.

Although she had been asked repeatedly by both Angel and Zach, she had claimed she wanted to go with them, but Angel and Zach had both been worried about her condition. Zach thought she needed a good breakfast. Angel thought she needed a home.

''Of course, Anna's going,'' Zach said. ''My mother is entrusting her to me. I'm just sending you two along first. I've got some business to take care of.''

"Zach!''

The man behind Angel pushed his suitcase and a plastic gift shop bag inches forward, as if he thought his luggage might persuade them to conclude their business.

"Sir, there's no seats on the flight to Fiji,'' the agent interrupted, leaning across the counter. "While you're deciding on your destination and the number of people in your party, would you mind stepping aside so that I can help these other customers?''

Muttering an apology, Angel and Zach walked over to the concourse.

"Zach, I'm leaving town, your sister's leaving town. That means your plans are up in the air. You can't mean that you're staying.''

"Angel, I'll come later. Please take my sister. Get her out of here.''

"Zach, don't do this to me,'' Angel pleaded. "I don't want to leave without you.''

"I can't go, Angel, you know that. I'm a wanted man. I shot my brother and I'm a material witness to a double homicide.''

"I saw the same murders,'' she hissed, and then brought her voice down low as several travelers turned to stare. "I should be staying, too.''

"You can't identify the automatic rifle Isabel used

or her outfit or even the position from which she shot. I'm much more useful.''

He didn't add that the reason why she wasn't as good a witness as he was was precisely because she had done as he had asked—hit the ground immediately, and with no arguing about doing what he told her or not.

He figured he would be willing to argue with her for the rest of her life about who was boss, about who was too old-fashioned, about who was living in the wrong century—as long as he could know that in matters of life and death, they would trust each other.

Without question or doubt.

But this wasn't a life-or-death moment. This was getting on a plane. And Angel was being stubborn.

''So give a statement to the police this afternoon,'' Angel insisted. ''We'll leave this evening. Together. All three of us.''

''It'll take more than that. If O'Malley was so quick to judge me guilty you can imagine that others will be even quicker and even more sure of themselves.''

''Then let's all stay and we'll work through it. Together.''

''No, because every day we stay the piranhas who work with my family and yours will try to pull us into the business. Just like my father said.''

"I don't want to go by myself."

"You'll be taking care of Anna. And I will come. I really will."

She shook her head.

"We can't win, can we?"

"No, but it's best if you leave first," Zach said, reaching up to push a lock of hair away from her face. "Take care of my sister. I'll come when I can. I'm sure it'll get straightened out."

"This is like Las Vegas."

"No, Angel, it's not like Las Vegas. This time I'll be there. You have to be patient."

"I'm fresh out of patience," she said. "I want my husband."

He consoled her with a kiss and then a long hug. But in his heart, he didn't know how long it would be before he would see her again.

He only knew one thing—she was strong enough that he could rely on her to care for Anna, to protect her. She was a woman of substance, not a child anymore.

"Going somewhere?" a gravelly voice said.

Zach abruptly relinquished Angel.

"O'Malley, what are you doing here?"

"I could ask the same of you."

Zach looked to make sure Anna was safe. His mother had seated herself next to her and they talked quietly and earnestly.

"Mr. O'Malley, let us go," Angel said. "We just want some peace."

"Let's have a talk first."

THEY FOUND A QUIET bench at the nearest food concessionaire. The waitress served them sodas and O'Malley laid a tape recorder out on the table.

"Start with when you left my office," he ordered Zach. "I know you're not a liar, but don't protect anybody by leaving anything out. Come clean, Zach. Clean as snow. It's the only way."

Zach began talking. He stopped only when the waitress brought back refills and when O'Malley had to switch the tape. And then only long enough to drink some soda and catch his breath.

After a full half hour, during which neither O'Malley nor Angel said a word, Zach closed with an explanation of why he left the Martin home even as the Glencoe police responded to Anna's call.

"I didn't want Angel or Anna being taken in for questioning," he concluded. "I've told you everything. They don't know any more than I do."

O'Malley sighed.

"All right, you've given me a lot," he said, flipping the recorder off. "There's only one thing wrong with this story."

"What's that?" Zach said.

O'Malley closed his eyes, blinking back tears.

"Guy was my son," he said. "Lord help me, he was my son."

Angel gasped.

"But...but how could that be?"

"I dated Jeanne many years ago, on the sly because she was supposed to be Tony's girl. I didn't have anything to offer her, but Lord, how I loved her. She wanted to marry, but I said no. It wasn't the time for it."

"I think I can see what's coming," Zach said mournfully.

"I bet you can. I wanted to finish law school because I knew a Bridgeport guy with no family and no education had no future. I had nothing. I didn't realize how urgent her request was until she broke it off with Sciopelli, turned around and married your father. And then Guy showed up and I knew."

"Did Angel's father know?"

"Yeah, and that's why I could never truly go full throttle on him, although I hated him, pardon me, Angel, but I did. And I felt something very close to gratitude to your father, Zach, for marrying your mother and raising my son. My only son. It was only as the years wore on that I wished I could claim him."

"Why didn't you?"

"Your mother was afraid of how it would affect you and Anna—and I was afraid it would kill my career and my chances of busting up organized crime in this city.''

"So you kept this a complete secret?"

"Yes. She occasionally called me for little favors, getting Guy out of jail for his problems with the law, calling for you when no one would give you a job on the up-and-up. I had some contact with Guy, met him a few times in very casual circumstances, and I kept thinking that he'd turn around. I didn't know it would end like this. He never knew that I loved him. I think if he had known, it might have been easier.''

"I'm sorry," Zach said.

Angel reached out and took O'Malley's wrinkled hand in her own.

"Aw, hell," O'Malley said, and wiped his eyes with his napkin. "Look, Zach, you've given me a lot to work with. So I'm going to give you a little something. Three tickets.''

He laid out three ticket folders on the table.

"A little cash," he said, adding a fourth plain business-size envelope to the pile. "And the equivalent of two baby albums.''

Thump! Angel's file folder and a second, thicker folder that could only be Zach's.

"Your mother has agreed to testify about your father's activities," O'Malley said. "And Interpol has already set to work on nailing Isabel—we think she's a professional who's been involved in a number of other murders. And Salvatore is going to dissolve the Sciopelli and Martin companies.''

"How is he?" Angel asked.

"A little shell-shocked, but he'll recover. He had no idea about Isabel. Mr. Martin set him up to be introduced to her at the Christmas party—that was her entrée to your family. Salvatore didn't know that she didn't feel the same way he did."

"What's he going to do now?"

"He's promised complete cooperation. He's opened the study to us. He really doesn't have the heart or the head to continue the business. Point is, we won't need your help anymore to take apart the crime syndicate your fathers have put together."

"So where are we going?" Zach asked, fingering the tickets.

"Why not let me surprise you?" O'Malley suggested. "By the way, your flight leaves at one o'clock."

"O'Malley, that's only ten minutes from now!" Angel exclaimed.

"Then we won't have time for a sloppy, sentimental goodbye, will we?"

Zach scooped up the tickets, the cash and the file folders.

"Oh, Zach?"

"Yeah, O'Malley?"

"Through it all, you've always been the son I

wished I had had. When your mother called me and asked me to give you a chance, I had my doubts. But I've come to respect you. Lord forgive me, I've come to really love you."

"Feeling's mutual," Zach murmured.

O'Malley glanced at Angel. "You did the right thing leaving. You wouldn't have any part of it when a lot of other people might have turned a blind eye. Both of you are good people—I'm gonna miss you."

"I guess I'm going to miss you, too," Angel allowed. "In an odd kind of way."

"I thought there weren't going to be any sloppy, sentimental goodbyes," Zach teased, reaching out to touch O'Malley's shoulder.

"Oh, yeah, right," he snarled good-naturedly. "Get the hell out here, kids."

Angel laughed and kissed him on the forehead.

Then they ran out of the food court to pick up Anna.

"Come on, we got ten minutes to get to gate B-11," Zach urged.

"Uh, Zach, I've got something to tell you," Anna said.

Mrs. Martin put her arm around Anna.

"Anna really doesn't want to go," she said. "She would because she loves you, but..."

"But I'm not ready for the whole world," Anna

spoke up. "I'm pretty good just where I am, in my own house. I would miss it very much."

Zach nodded, understanding.

"I'll come back," he said. He put his arm around Angel. "We'll come back. But it will be a long time before we can do that. Can you remember that we love you that long?"

Anna nodded bravely.

"Run to your flight," Mrs. Martin said. "I'll remind her, I'll remind both of us, whenever we almost forget."

They exchanged quick hugs and suppressed tears and then Angel and Zach sprinted to the gate.

They turned around to see O'Malley slipping his arms around Zach's mother. Anna waved.

"They make a wonderful pair."

"Angel, I think they have a long way to go before we can call them a couple."

"It'll happen," she said confidently.

"Oh, come on, Angel, we'll never make it!" Zach exclaimed.

They got to the gate just as the agent was closing the door, but she smiled when she took their tickets and checked the passports O'Malley had thoughtfully included.

Angel and Zach took their seats in first class. The pilot announced that Flight 427 nonstop to Paris was departing shortly.

"We're going to Paris?"

"City of lovers," Zach said. "That O'Malley's no fool."

"Mr. Martin?" the stewardess asked.

The couple looked up warily.

"Yes?"

"I need to check your passports. Sorry, it's regulations."

The couple exchanged nervous glances, but gave up their passports.

"Everything looks in order," the stewardess said, slipping them back two new passport folders.

Puzzled, Angel opened hers.

Her picture was the same, but she now had her name back—Jennifer Smith.

And a quick peek at Zach's confirmed that he had been given a new identity, too.

"Mr. O'Malley ordered a bottle of champagne to be chilled for you," the stewardess continued. "Would you like me to serve you after takeoff?"

"Champagne would be nice," Zach said. If O'Malley set up their escape route, Zach wasn't going to question it.

"He said that you've just gotten married," the stewardess continued. "Congratulations."

The stewardess walked away to help a passenger with his baggage before Zach or Angel could thank her.

Zach looked at Angel with a mischievous glint in his eyes. He reached out and unclasped the fragile chain around her neck, producing the ring he had given her ten years before.

He slipped it onto her left ring finger.

"Yes," he said. "We're finally married. In our own way."

"Yes, finally."

"Jennifer," he said, feeling the smooth syllables of her name on his tongue. "That's a very pretty name. We're going to get married in Paris, you know."

She pursed her lips.

"I mean, we should get married in Paris," he amended.

She pulled the in-flight magazine from the seat in front of them and studied the cover as if there was going to be a test on it.

"Would you marry me in Paris?"

She looked at him and gave him a heart-stopping smile.

"Are you asking me or telling me to marry you?"

"Oh, Angel, I mean, Jennifer, I've learned my lesson. I'm never telling you to do anything ever again. Or, at least, not too often. But you'll have to teach this sixteenth-century man how to do it."

He grinned at her, the grin that made most women

in the world forgive him his charming but bossy demeanor.

She stuck her face into the magazine. "I think you can figure this one out on your own."

"All right, I'm asking you, very respectfully, very lovingly, to get married in Paris."

She put down the magazine slowly. He noticed there were tears softening the cotton candy blue of her eyes.

"I'd be delighted to marry you, Mr....what did you say your name was?"

"Bob. Robert Smith," Zach said, glancing one more time at his passport.

"It's very convenient that we have the same last name. Maybe O'Malley meant for us to consider ourselves already married. I know I have."

"We're still getting married. Official-like. I don't want anything more to come between us," he said. "Because I've waited too long for this. I love you, Angel."

"Jennifer," she corrected. "And I love you, too...Bob."

"I'll tell the stewardess that champagne would be very nice. We need to celebrate."

He kissed his new bride full on the mouth just as the engines roared to life and the plane sped down the runway toward their new future.

Epilogue

CHICAGO (UPI)—Reputed mob boss Guy Martin, Sr., was found dead Thursday morning in his lakeside home in the affluent Chicago suburb of Glencoe. According to a family spokesman, the cause of death was an accidental overdose of the medication prescribed to control the pain he endured during chemotherapy treatments for stage-four metastasized lung cancer. Mr. Martin had recently dismissed his private nurse and was home alone at the time of his death.

Mr. Martin is survived by his wife and two of his children. Private services will be held at the Sacred Heart Cathedral on Tower Road in Winnetka.

Hours before his death, Mr. Martin had been informed of the murder of his eldest son, Guy Martin, Jr. Guy, Jr., is widely believed to have been the victim of a struggle for power over trafficking in prostitution, drugs and gambling, which took the lives of Tony and Antoinette Sciopelli at a north suburban restaurant. No suspects have been arrested in the case. The Chicago police department said that the investigation has been turned over to the district attorney's office, who will work with federal and international law enforcement agencies to solve this series of brutal murders.

Interpol has reported that it is stepping up its search for a professional assassin who may have been involved in the slaying of Guy, Jr., the murders of Antoinette and Tony Sciopelli as well as two sons and a daughter-in-law. The assailant is described as a white female, approximately five-ten, dark-haired and has worked in the past as a runway model in Europe. She has been implicated in a number of assassinations of leading businessmen in Moscow and Prague.

At this afternoon's press conference, District Attorney Patrick O'Malley indicated that his office would vigorously press charges against any wrongdoers in the recent tragedies of the Sciopelli and Martin families.

But he added that he had received the cooperation of Martin's widow as well as the surviving Sciopelli son. With their help, he has received sufficient information to lead him to believe that the murders of Guy Martin, Jr., and the recently murdered Sciopelli family members marked the end of a struggle for power over Chicago's criminal underworld.

Younger son Salvatore Sciopelli, still in mourning, has agreed to cooperate fully in any further investigations. He will reportedly oversee the dissolution of the Sciopelli Construction Company and has expressed plans to devote himself to the construction of buildings on the grounds of Sacred Heart Cathedral.

This marks a violent end to the Winnetka Shopping Mall project, a multimillion dollar shopping center that was to infuse the small suburb with much-needed tax revenues. The mayor of Winnetka announced at a press conference today that a new industrial park will be built on that property.

"Chicago is a tough town," O'Malley said at the conclusion of the press conference. "But I am determined to make this a safe place in which our children can grow. While I am in office, there will be a vigorous pursuit of wrongdoers."

Mr. O'Malley would not comment on reports that an attorney in his office, the surviving son

of Guy Martin, Sr., has left the country, reportedly in the company of the only daughter
of the Sciopelli family.

Welcome to *Love Inspired*™

A brand-new series of contemporary inspirational love stories.

Join men and women as they learn valuable lessons about facing the challenges of today's world and about life, love and faith.

**Look for the following March 1998
Love Inspired™ titles:**

CHILD OF HER HEART
by Irene Brand

A FATHER'S LOVE
by Cheryl Wolverton

WITH BABY IN MIND
by Arlene James

Available in retail outlets in February 1998.

LIFT YOUR SPIRITS AND GLADDEN YOUR HEART
with *Love Inspired!*™

Steeple
Hill™

LI398

Born in the USA

**Look for these titles—
available at your favorite retail outlet!**

January 1998
Renegade Son by Lisa Jackson

Danielle Summers had problems: a rebellious child
and unscrupulous enemies. In addition, her Montana
ranch was slowly being sabotaged. And then there was
Chase McEnroe—who admired her land and desired her
body. But Danielle feared he would invade more than just
her property—he'd trespass on her heart.

February 1998
The Heart's Yearning by Ginna Gray

Fourteen years ago Laura gave her baby up for adoption,
and not one day had passed that she didn't think about
him and agonize over her choice—so she finally followed
her heart to Texas to see her child. But the plan to watch
her son from afar doesn't quite happen that way, once the
boy's sexy—*single*—father takes a decided interest in *her*.

March 1998
First Things Last by Dixie Browning

One look into Chandler Harrington's dark eyes and
Belinda Massey could refuse the Virginia millionaire nothing.
So how could the no-nonsense nanny believe the rumors that
he had kidnapped his nephew—an adorable, healthy little boy
who crawled as easily into her heart as he did into her lap?

**BORN IN THE USA: Love, marriage—
and the pursuit of family!**

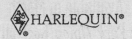

Not The Same Old Story!

Exciting, glamorous romance stories that take readers around the world.

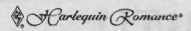
Sparkling, fresh and tender love stories that bring you pure romance.

Bold and adventurous— Temptation is strong women, bad boys, great sex!

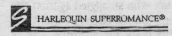
Provocative and realistic stories that celebrate life and love.

Contemporary fairy tales—where anything is possible and where dreams come true.

Heart-stopping, suspenseful adventures that combine the best of romance and mystery.

LOVE & LAUGHTER™
Humorous and romantic stories that capture the lighter side of love.

Look us up on-line at: http://www.romance.net   HGENERIC

Available in March
from *New York Times* bestselling author

ELIZABETH LOWELL

Carlson Raven had no choice but to rescue Janna Morgan—
the beautiful, courageous woman who struggled against the
stormy sea. When he pulled her from the choppy waters and
revived her with the heat of his body, his yearning was as
unexpected as it was enduring.

But Carlson was as untamed and enigmatic as the sea he
loved. Would Janna be the woman to capture his wild and
lonely heart?

LOVE SONG FOR A RAVEN

Available in March 1998
wherever books are sold.